He's coming. Mojo DeCanne.

A gust of wind parts the snow long enough for me to glimpse him standing there, dressed in a turn of the century suit. His wide-brimmed hat covers his eyes. He raises a crooked finger and wags it back and forth at me in a scolding motion. After a moment, his tongue slowly protrudes from his mouth, catching snowflakes with it like a child might. His tongue drips with blood, which stains the snow, then seems to grow longer, extending a few inches before I hear his laughter. With his snake-like tongue shimmering and slick with ice and crimson, he walks closer to the building with a long, eerie gait, until I am no longer able to see him from my vantage point.

But I can still hear him.

The door down in the lobby sounds as it opens then closes.

Footsteps, slow and deliberate, plod up the stairs…one by one.

"Gina." His voice is childlike but horrifying all at once. "Gina," he says again, only this time it's the voice of a demon.

Trembling uncontrollably, I move toward the door and look into the peephole.

He's crouched over, his tongue lapping the hole. As I stagger back I scream, "Daniel! Daniel!" And yet my voice sounds so small, as if I barely made any sound at all. The door rattles. The knob turns. Something comes through the keyhole, pink, wet and serpent-like, and I can hear him laughing again, his breath heavy and gurgling on the other side of the thin door that separates us. The tongue spirals towards me, curling, seeming to reach for me, wanting to wrap itself around my neck.

Something coils around my throat, thick and wet as it tightens and chokes me, pulls me down into a cold and never-ending darkness.

MANHATTAN GRIMOIRE

by Sandy DeLuca

Dedicated to Gianna.

May you always follow your heart.

ACKNOWLEDGMENTS

I want to thank David Niall Wilson and David Dodd for their kindness and professionalism. I am excited that my out-of-print titles will once again be made available to the public. I also want to thank Greg F. Gifune for believing in my work. Most of all, thank you to my readers.

1

It's always the same, this dream of my sister. She's in a church speaking to another woman in a low, otherworldly language. The woman with her has dark mystical eyes and skin the color of mahogany. Though I have no idea who this woman is, she is obviously connected somehow to my sister in a very meaningful way.

As she moves from my sister's side, the woman screams, runs to a window and presses her hands against the glass. She leaves bloody prints there as her sadness penetrates me and darkness falls over the entire scene. She whispers my name, *Gina*, in a voice that is somehow sweet, inviting and terrifying all at once.

I had the dream again this morning and couldn't get back to sleep. I never can once I've had it.

I get out of bed and bend down to kiss my boyfriend, not waiting to see if he opens his eyes. I put on a pair of jeans, an old sweatshirt and boots then grab my old fake fur from the closet. I slip a small digital camera into my pocket, walk down three flights of stairs with only a twenty-five watt bulb shedding dim light on the stairway. I should've packed a thirty-five millimeter, a powerful flash and some high-speed film. I should have waited until daylight, but predawn is when things waver in cracked window frames and when dark shadows spiral up from gutters and dank cellars. It's when the things I need to see and sense and feel are still awake.

I walk three blocks in freezing weather to the lot where I park my car. The streets are nearly empty, but for yellow cabs cruising by looking for early fares emerging from hotels. Police cars are parked randomly about, perhaps spying on deals going down in arched doorways, perhaps waiting for tired hookers to materialize from dark alleys. They pay no attention to my old Ford Escort. I feel innocuous and invisible, a subtle thread weaving through a concrete jungle where people dark and terrifying are hunted.

I drive as though I'm in a dream and before long find myself in Harlem. This one street in particular, empty, forsaken, and vile gives me the creeps every time I visit it. The brownstones here have been boarded up for years, the windows broken and the walls covered with graffiti, aging paint sprawled across cracked brick. The stink of lives gone bad hangs in the air. Random homeless sleep in these buildings, and dealers deal.

Despite the evil I sense so strongly here, I can't stay away. I come here after the dreams, after the beautiful black woman calls my name.

The church is nestled between a rundown Laundromat and a gutted bodega. I've seen shadowy things perched on its roof, mocking me before fading into early morning fog. The moon, not quite gone yet, reflects along the church's iron banisters, and sparkles amidst shadows twisting and slowly turning like surreal serpents trapped in brick and cement. Wild vines form intricate patterns as they slither over steps and windows, and I realize that every time I come here I see something new, something more. I've photographed nearly all the old neighborhoods and buildings in this city, but none leave me feeling the way this old church does. Although I've taken thousands of photographs of this place—inside and out—and even did a show in Chelsea last summer with some of the shots, you'd think I'd get my fill. But I haven't. And until I find my kid sister's body and figure out exactly what the hell happened here, I never will. For now, there's much more for me to capture, so many compositions and designs I've yet to find through the lens of my cameras, so many clues and answers I've yet to come across.

I slow down in front of the crumbling building. A nearby sign tells me *Jesus Saves*.

He never saved me, never saved my sister.

They found her bloody clothing in this church. Her blood stained the marble floor, but they never found her body. There were two others dead, lying on the altar, their hearts cut out and their eyes gazing toward a wooden crucifix someone had turned upside down.

The city is coming awake all around me…slowly, gradually.

It's Saturday. I don't have to work. I can go back to my apartment, crawl between the covers and listen to the city, drift away as horns and sirens blare, as the neighbors argue and as my boyfriend Tony gets ready to bring his art down to Soho.

I watch the church a while longer but decide not to snap any photographs this time. It watches me too, and I wonder if it takes notice of me, records my visits somehow. Does it know I'm here?

Eventually the lure of warm bedcovers and Tony's arms wrapped tightly around me wins out, and I head back to the alleged safety of my apartment.

2

The sun casts orange light above the buildings as deep black turns to gray and a streetlight on the corner dims. I can see archways and windows of shabby brownstones where lovers once loved and children once laughed. A small group of women wearing straw hats and carrying prayer books climb the church stairs. The Grim Reaper– time– claimed their passion long ago, watched as culture and belief died here. The sorrow is overwhelming, and I want to be consumed by the church standing vigil on this cracked and broken part of town. I want to die inside its musty walls and fall to Hell where demons celebrate the darkness inside me.

I ask the daylight to tear these thoughts from me, and as the sun rises higher, it does.

I consider photographing this sunrise in an attempt to show how its warm rays spread over the city, shedding light on even its most desolate corners. But I don't. Instead, I watch quietly and decide to go walking later, when Canal and Broadway spring to life and vendors line the walks with their wares, when Asian merchants stand in wait as people pluck rhinestone pins, sequined slippers and knockoff bags from hooks and shelves. I love to walk the strip from Canal to the Strand Bookstore, where I usually sift through stacks of vintage books on art and exotic cooking.

Though my plans are now set, I need to sleep first. I can only hope the dreams won't continue to haunt me. I turn the ignition, listen to the aged engine spark to life then I glance in the rear-view mirror. Blue and white lights flash as a black Crown Victoria pulls up behind me. Its door opens quickly and footsteps clack on gritty cement. Knuckles wrap hard on my window. I look up.

Detective Harris studies me, stoic and purposeful. His skin is smooth, light brown. His hair is longer than the last time I saw him, when he told me they'd found my sister's blood on clothing, on the floor, in the old church, in the days he'd come by to say they hadn't found her body yet. He'd asked so many questions. Did I remember anything? Who were her friends? Where did she go after work? He'd stopped coming around, stopped asking questions months ago, but still called now and then, assuring me the case was still open, and I know the questions haven't stopped in his head, just like they haven't stopped in mine.

His hair is soft and black, curling at his collar. He doesn't smile, merely shakes his head and I think he's beautiful as he motions for me to roll down the window. Once it's down he crouches low so we're face to face. His eyes darken and he begins to speak slowly, solemnly, telling me this particular street in Harlem is no place for me to be, especially alone, especially at this hour. He shakes his finger like a reprimanding parent, and I notice a small ring on his index finger that holds a black stone within a silver serpent. "I've seen you here before," he tells me. "You shouldn't do this."

My face flushes. His beauty embarrasses me. "I take pictures. That's all. Harlem fascinates me—all the neighborhoods do, I—"

"If it's pictures you want, Harlem's got plenty of material in good safe neighborhoods." He smiles slightly. "Take pictures of The Apollo. Go to Saint Nicolas Park. Snap some shots of the old Cotton Club. There's good stuff in those places. Don't come here." He shakes his head again. "Besides, it's not just pictures you're looking for."

I hold his stare but say nothing.

"She's not in that church, Gina."

His gaze flickers toward the old building. "I searched it from top to bottom. She's not there."

My eyes fill with tears. "I know."

He's looking at me again. He narrows his eyes, stands. "Go back Downtown." He backs away, turns in silence then glances toward the top of the church.

I wonder if he sees the phantoms I've seen.

I watch him get into his unmarked car, but I know he won't drive away until I do. He'll follow me for a while until he's satisfied I'm far enough from this place, so I put the car in drive and move away slowly. I cut in and out of several streets until I'm on Fifth Avenue.

Black couples walk the avenue, wheeling baby carriages, carrying Styrofoam cups. Young men are gathering at bodegas. Old men tap canes on stained sidewalks, glare at graffiti on brick. Harlem is alive with its beauty, its people proud, resilient and often tragic. It's a place of diversity, history, jazz, art, and energy. Its dark places go into hiding on a morning like this, slip into oblivion and life is lived to its fullest here in the open. Death is a silent watcher in shadow, in places like that church.

I look into my rear-view mirror. The detective is still behind me, stays there until I reach the Guggenheim and then disappears into a cacophony of taxis and delivery trucks. I wonder if he has a wife or girlfriend, if it's tough for him to love anybody because his hands are always bloody, because death is always one step away. And even if there is someone, does he remain lonely because the filth and decadence of the city possess him, because his soul belongs to *it* and his heart is buried in the dirt with the dead?

I can't think about that now though. I've got things to do. I've demons of my own to wrestle.

3

I climb the stairs as shards of light guide me upward. I slip the camera from my pocket and photograph abstract patterns sunrays make on the old wooden steps, but soon realize I need to catch my breath, so I rest against the banister for a moment. The elevator broke last summer. The super promised he'd fix it, but just like everything else—the broken windows, the front door that doesn't lock, and the leaky faucets—it never gets done. There's always liquor on the super's breath. He lives in a damp room off the downstairs hallway and resembles the rats I've seen scurrying across the yard.

Detective Harris came here to see him a few times. I heard them talking outside my window and the super's slurred words, "Nobody ever came around. I heard everything since the elevator broke, every footstep on those stairs. Ain't nobody been around."

I think about Detective Harris climbing rafters in the old church or descending into its bowels. I wonder what else he found, if horrible things peered at him from dark corners, if ancient and evil relics lay hidden there. Is he saving somebody from evil now? Is he an angel looking out for me?

Tony's awake. I hear him singing something by Bob Dylan, asking how it feels to be all alone.

He greets me at the door. His eyes are sleepy, his hair tousled. There's something on his mind. He looks right through me when he speaks, "I made coffee. It's still hot."

"Are you hungry? I could cook." I walk past him really not caring if he's hungry. I'm thinking about the detective, about the woman in my dreams. I'm wondering where my sister's bones are buried.

It feels as though Tony's a ghost, a wisp of someone I once loved, or never loved at all and thought was someone else. I don't feel anything, not even when he fucks me. I wonder if he knows. I wonder if he believes I still want him. I always tell myself it's the last time, but I don't leave. I exist instead inside this shell of a life we've created.

He accepts my indifference, probably thinks it's because of what happened to my sister. Maybe it is—maybe— "See you tonight." He plucks keys from the table and glides away like an apparition, like something I've imagined. But he can't be a dream, can he? My dreams are more vivid than he is.

I listen to his footsteps on the stairs, thankful he's left me alone.

In the beginning, I thought he was an enigma, a challenge. I was attracted to his arrogance, the way he ignored me when I strolled into GiGi's in The Bowery. Everyone else looked at me, the girl with wild red-gold hair, lean and firm wearing Egyptian jewelry and leopard boots, the hip photographer who'd been published in countless independent rags, whose work adorns low rent offices downtown and galleries on the fringes of the elite. A girl who makes no money at it and still needs to work fulltime in a stiff office and every day when she awakens tells herself it's killing her, but goes on because she must serve her prison term, must slave for a check at week's end, must poison her creativity and one day be buried in a plot no one will visit.

It's a bitch holding onto artistic vision without giving in to temptation. I don't want my work to match the theme of some rich yuppie's game room; don't want it to look cute or fashionable. I'd be selling out if I did. I'd lose my fucking soul. It makes you hungry, brings you to places most people don't want to be, and makes people say you're eccentric.

I used to tour lower Manhattan bars before Tony moved in— before my sister disappeared—seeking thrills, playing mind games with men, growing tired when they became too needy. I can be cold, uncaring. In the back of my mind, in a foggy fantasy, I've left someone dead in an alley, walked away with his blood on my boot. Maybe I blocked its memory because what I've done is so heinous, but deep down I know it's just a guilt dream, not real, an evil thing in my soul.

Sometimes I think I'm a sociopath. My sister told me it's my Venus in Scorpio. I think it's a glitch in my brain, something my mother planted there when I was conceived, an uncontrollable imagination that brings me to places I wouldn't dare go in the flesh, introducing me to lovers I'll never love and to bloody scenes I invent in my mind's eye. Tony was merely a dream man, someone aloof living in a bohemian subculture I've always been too timid to adopt, so I used to play out bed scenes with him in a special corner of my head. It was safe, a handy façade like my fake mink jackets, spider necklaces and platinum wigs.

I watched Tony for weeks. He never left GiGi's alone, but he did his drinking in silence. Perhaps he created paintings in his mind, deciding whether to use oils or acrylics, whether to stretch the canvas or not. Before last call he'd choose his nightly lover, blonde, brunette or redhead, it didn't matter. They all had need etched on their faces, but one night a woman that looked like my sister, Allie was her name, left hanging on his arm. I was angry for a moment, though I knew it wasn't her. She was still nursing wounds from her recent breakup with a guy named Ronnie Bateman. And even if it was Allie she didn't know I'd fallen in love with the painter who sold his wares in Soho on Saturdays and Sundays, who spent his weekdays in a crumbling studio loft making art, making love to women who found him incredible, women he disposed of like ruined paint brushes.

Each night at GiGi's I imagined sending him notes on damp napkins and drinks in frosty glasses and perhaps a package of condoms.

He slid dark glasses to the tip of his nose and glanced at me once or twice, as if he sensed the attraction. On the night I took him home the air in GiGi's felt different, as though I'd walked over a threshold, maybe because I was dressed in black, a silver belt draped casually around my waist, my eyes lined with kohl. Maybe because I felt dark, dangerous and sexy. I drank whisky straight up as a drag queen giggled beside me and a man wearing a toupee and sucking on a toothpick asked me to dance. Tony merely stared into space, tapped his foot to the music. His hair was long then, cascading down his back in light brown waves. He wore dark glasses even at night. One evening when old disco music blasted through the club and drag queens filled the dance floor, I had a drink sent to him at the bar. My hands shook, my stomach felt sour. I'd crossed the boundary from fantasy to reality.

The waitress set the drink down in front of him then nodded in my direction when he said something soft and low in her ear. The drink was bourbon. He eyed it, ran his finger over the glass rim then took a deep swig. He wiped his lips and looked my way. I couldn't see his eyes, and his dark lenses sparkled as strobe lights flickered above. He smiled knowingly, rose from his seat and made his way to the restroom.

On his way back he came up behind me and asked if I was waiting for someone. The whiskey had made me bold, uncaring, and I told him I'd been waiting for him. Out of the blue I asked, "Did you fuck Allie?"

A man with black hair like Detective Harris's, wearing an old-fashioned waistcoat and pants slid into a nearby seat. His skin was dark and he wore a diamond earring. He plucked a beer bottle from the bar and took a long pull, his eyes locked on Tony and me. I noticed a strange tattoo on his hand, a red spider set on a pile of bones.

Tony glanced at him and nodded. He smiled slightly then he turned back to me. "Don't know anyone by that name."

The man seemed amused, but he gave me a sick feeling in my gut.

"She may have lied to you, told you another name."

The liquor was giving me a headache. The man began to look like a demon I'd seen in an old surreal painting. His eyes narrowed and drool trickled down his chin. Tony seemed more dangerous, suddenly, his eyes hardening. But it didn't scare me. I wanted him no matter what.

He moved closer. "What's it matter anyway? You're taking me home, right?"

"Yeah." I wondered again if it was my sister who'd hung on his arm, kissed his cheek through blue smoke, wrapped her sequined shawl around her shoulders and tossed her hair as his hand slipped to her waist. She'd never admit it when she was alive. Now she won't confess it in dreams when she comes to me from her secret burial plot. Tony would never tell me the truth either.

Other people joined the man at the bar, all were dressed in old clothes, their arms and legs bent at odd angles and their eyes void of emotion. Strange tattoos, inverted crosses and bloody knives, stretched across hues of cinnamon flesh. Tony didn't notice; he just kept talking to me, using his charm. "I just got evicted, couldn't swing the rent on a street artist's income." He told me that the first night. My heart leapt at the thought of taking him home and keeping him like some stray cat.

Lately my fascination has diminished to say the least. I've been wondering what made me think he was so exalted before he came here, so unapproachable. He's just a guy, a bum who's living off me.

I want to sleep, dream of the woman. Perhaps she'll tell me where to find her, where to find Allie's rotting flesh. Maybe the detective is parked on the street below looking up at my apartment, wanting to come inside. Maybe we can dream together. The cop and dream woman are my lovers in fantasies, and Allie is whole, smoking clove cigarettes on the front stairs, drinking hot coffee and smiling when our voices float through the window.

I want to call Detective Harris, ask him if he knows more than he's telling. But I don't, and try to sleep instead. I slip between white sheets, glance a moment at empty pill bottles by my nightstand. I think about Dr. McKinley and the appointments I never kept. She made me uncomfortable, prying into my past.

The last session with her brought me over the edge and I remember thinking, this is the last fucking time I'm coming here.

She sat before me, so stoic in a plain gray suit, hands clasped in her lap. Her eyes were the color of her suit. They seem to condemn me when she asked, "Maybe this isn't all about your sister, maybe there's more. Do you wonder about your mother? Do you think perhaps she was mentally ill and that your father kept it from you? Don't you wonder, Gina?"

"She just left, decided she didn't want a family, didn't love us." My voice was harsh. Who the fuck was this woman to accuse my father of deceit? Images of my mother haunted me at that moment. Her face white, horror etched across it as she waved her hands. Her words were senseless. "Don't you see them? They live here now. They'll come to you too, Gina. Wait, you'll see."

Dr. McKinley studied me for a moment. "You need to confront the truth about your mother and yourself." She leaned forward, her eyes grew dark, more accusing. "I think deep down inside you want to know." She took a prescription pad from her desk, scribbled on it and then slid white paper towards me. "You need to stay on the medication and you need to see me more than once a month. Have the receptionist book an appointment for next week. If we haven't made progress in another month, then we'll talk about hospitalization."

Her pills took away my dreams of Allie, of the black woman. I need them too much. Tony told me a good therapist wouldn't have been so blunt, that she sounded like a quack. So, I'll figure it out myself. It's time to move ahead, to resurrect what's been dead inside me. I close my eyes and pray for sweet slumber.

4

I couldn't sleep, so I walked to Soho, blending with tourists and weekend shoppers.

Broadway is a nightmare. Men dressed in worn army coats sell bootleg movies and silver jewelry from makeshift stands while eyeing passersby with hollow faces. There are things on rooftops no one else sees but me, creatures from Hell that spring down on innocents upon command from the Devil. I've seen them; slithering and scurrying above since I was little, and I've always wondered if I'm one of their offspring. Why else would I be able to see them?

I accidentally step on a vendor's foot while crossing. He curses at me. I ignore him and make my way to a corner store where silver chains hang from rusty hooks. A butterfly necklace catches my eye. An Asian man quickly grabs it and says, "You want? Ten dollar."

"Eight," I answer as someone brushes my shoulder, someone tall, with skin the color of rich mahogany, hair braided with red and silver beads. She turns. It's the black woman from my dreams. She's standing there, looking at my feet. She walks towards me, bends, gracefully straightens, looks me in the eye, "Is this yours?" She's holding a silver hoop earring.

"Yes, the hook is loose, keeps falling. Thank you." I notice her jewelry, wooden beads, serpents carved from ivory and blood red stones.

The Asian man frantically waves the necklace, "Eight dollar."

We ignore him. His voice becomes faint. He's merely a silhouette existing in another world.

The woman tips her head to one side. The beads in her hair make soft clicking sounds. "Want your fortune told? I read over on Canal Street, next to the paint store." The serpents on a chain around her neck seem to move, rear their heads in my direction, spiral out with pointed fangs. I back away as a hissing noise erupts. "Maybe," I say as serpents slither against her flesh, prick a pulsing vein. Red droplets trickle across her beautiful skin.

"You OK?" she asks.

I blink my eyes. It's just a necklace. There's no blood. I'm so fucking tired.

She smiles. Her lips are moist, luscious. "I tell fortunes every Saturday for a while, other times I'm over in Harlem. I need to tend to my son. It's a bitch, you know." She studies my face. "Bye, then."

"Good bye." My voice is so soft I don't even know if she heard me.

She terrifies me, but I want to follow her. She knows secrets, my secrets.

On impulse, I remove the camera from my pocket, snap her picture as she backs away. She giggles. Her laughter is like a song I've heard in my dreams.

I turn onto Canal. The crowd chokes me, voices frighten me. I search in vain for the fortuneteller. The paint store is flanked by apartment buildings, people selling beaded purses, black umbrellas, and Picasso scarves. The things on rooftops lean over and glare at me with leering faces. I wonder if the woman was real. I can't find her. I want to cry. I'll never see her again except in exotic, horrifying dreams.

A girl crosses the street. She's wearing a sequined shawl. Her hair is red-gold like Allie's—like my own. I call to her. She turns. She's old, her face scarred with deep wrinkles. Her skin hangs from her neck.

A siren blares in the distance and I wish her away, leaving only smoke from a hotdog vendor's tinny oven where she once stood.

I walk to West Broadway. I want to see how Tony's doing, if he's sold anything. Maybe I'll bring him a cup of coffee and watch his paintings if he needs to duck into a restaurant to pee.

The streets always smell of ash and pigeon shit. The cement is filthy with steam rising from it, and it reminds me of a carnival on West Broadway between Prince and Spring. Street artists hang paintings on racks and grin as you pass by, hoping you'll stop to look at their work, perhaps even buy something so they can pay their rent or eat dinner that night. They're pathetic creatures from an impoverished subculture. Nonetheless, like forbidden sex, they fascinate me.

A photographer is spreading black and white photos of dancers on a portable table. His face lights up when I approach. I stop for a moment and he tells me his mother taught ballet back in Chicago, that he once worked for a glitzy music magazine. I wonder what his mother would think if she saw her son thin and pale, vending his work for so little, eyes, moist as light snow begins to gather on his torn jacket.

I walk to a spot where Tony normally sells his paintings. He's not here. I ask around. A woman dressed in threadbare pants and a patched sweater smiles at me. Her front teeth are rotting. She's leaning watercolor paintings against an empty building. "Haven't seen Tony since the summer," she says.

"I heard he had trouble with his father," says a woman with a Russian accent as she spreads tiny cat paintings on the walk.

"He never mentioned his father to me," I tell her.

"You don't need to know," she answers. I back away as her eyes narrow and seem to take on an eerie glow.

A group of abstract painters clustered in front of a deli tell me they heard he moved to the West Coast.

No one has seen him. No one.

How can he be so irresponsible? He's been telling me sales are bad, that things will get better as the holidays approach. Where the hell is he, with someone else? Or is he getting high in some obscure place in the city?

I decide I'm leaving him. This fucking does it. It hurts, kills me, but I can't go on like this. He's no good for me, and I don't need this shit.

I turn the corner, walk quickly down Prince Street. The rumble of the subway erupts and things hovering on rooftops explode with laughter. I look up and see a familiar face, the man who was at the bar on the night I took Tony home. Others gather around him. They point at me, mock me. I begin to run, bumping into people, slipping on the icy sidewalk. The rooftop beings take flight, hover above me as I hail a cab.

I slide into the back seat, sigh heavily as snow begins to come down hard.

"Where to, lady?" The driver is Middle Eastern. He's smiling. There's something off. His eyes seem dead. His hands barely touch the steering wheel as he slowly pulls away from the curb.

I give him my address, watching streets and buildings float by as he speeds away.

It's not long before the streets no longer look familiar to me. Maybe it's the snow coming down so hard, or maybe it's just fatigue. Maybe it's something else, something far deadlier.

I've got to sleep, got to get my head straight.

My eyes close.

I concentrate on the motion of the taxi, and wonder if this is the closest I'll come today.

5

This isn't right.
There's no traffic here.
I'd see headlights through the blinding snow if we'd driven down my street.

The driver slows down, his shoulders slumped and his hands gripping the steering wheel. The cab fishtails to the curb and I clutch the edge of the seat as we ease safely in Park. I think about how in an instant life can be snuffed out. I remember my father and want to weep.

At this moment, I want to be loved, I want to feel tender arms wrapped around me while the city transforms, while the elements bury the morning like a lost soul, a child who shined for a moment and was then consumed by the beauty of a white shimmering cloak. Now that soul seems lost in all this frigid numbness, changing by the moment with each drift, with each tiny flake of snow, and I find myself hypnotized by the steady stream of white crystals. Maybe that lost soul is me.

Eyes glaring at me in the rear-view mirror darken my thoughts. They're the eyes of a killer.

The driver turns, smiles slowly, "Your destination." Gone is the pleasant Middle Eastern man. The demon man who taunts me from rooftops, who sat at the bar on the night Tony came home with me has returned. He extends his hand to me, and blood drips from his fingertips. There's a knife in his palm. "I think this is yours."

"Fuck you." I wish him away, as I do when evil things whisper to me in the dark and awaken me from dreams. Lately, they come often.

"I'm still here, bitch," he says through ashen lips. The knife falls from his hand to my lap, smears my jeans with blood.

I push the blade off me, and as it falls to the floor and slides beneath the front seat, I wonder whose blood is on it. With fear overtaking me, I throw open the door and tumble from the cab. As my feet touch the icy walk they slip out from under me and I fall. I look up in time to see the cab disappear into a veil of thick snow. Smoke curls from its exhaust, laughter rumbles from its open window. I lie there a moment, shivering from cold and fear, then roll and crouch into a kneeling position and reach for the support of a nearby newsstand.

A single newspaper is predominantly displayed across the newsstand, its bold headline announcing a woman named Allie Roderick is still missing. Allie. My sister.

But there's no newsstand by my apartment. Where the hell am I?

My hands ache from the cold, and I remember that I left my gloves in the cab, long elegant black ones with sequins at the edges. My hair is soaked and droplets trickle beneath my collar onto the back of my neck. I blink, strain my eyes, and wave away blinding snow, then take a few steps, moving carefully so as not to fall again.

It's then that I realize I'm at the old church.

Its door is open, and music plays inside. I take two steps closer, and see someone standing in the doorway. A woman… the beautiful black woman…she's waving. She looks ethereal and magical because her hair glistens with countless diamonds—or is it just snow? Her skin shimmers as I move closer. "I've been waiting for you," she whispers. I want her to cradle me in her arms, to offer me her breasts so that my soul will be nourished. I want to be a babe safe in her womb, and I think if only I could die now, if only I could end this life and be reborn from her flesh, everything would be all right again.

She puts a finger to her lips, backs away and shuts the door.

"No," I cry to the storm, to the slate gray sky. "Wait!"

"Gina," a familiar voice says from somewhere behind me.

I turn quickly, lose my balance. My hands slap ice, and just as my legs begin to turn numb, two strong arms lift me back to my feet. "What in God's name are you doing out here? How'd you get here?"

Through the swirl of snow, I see Detective Harris scolding me, but I can think of nothing to say. I just stare at him, as if seeing him for the first time.

"Come on," he says, "I'll get you home. You need some coffee, something hot, you're shivering. There's blood on your hands and on your clothes. You've scrapped yourself."

"I'm fine," I say, suddenly able to find words. But the voice is not my own. It belongs to the woman that entered the church, whose body is warm and loved and new. "No coffee, thanks."

Now I'm in his car watching snow fall in heavy drifts. A blast of heat warms my hands and feet. Harris tells me to buckle up. He's silent as he pulls away from the curb and drives away slowly. A half dozen women dressed in black and walking in a single file seem to creep alongside empty buildings on this street. One of them peels back a scarf from her head and glares at me. She's not human.

A gasp dies in my throat.

The detective looks at me quickly then his attention is back to traffic and snow. He turns onto a busy avenue where people are streaming from small grocery stores with bags filled; supplies for the wintry day and night ahead, I imagine. They all look normal, not otherworldly like the people I just saw. A light changes to red and the detective looks at me again. "Something startle you back there, Gina?"

"Those people."

He rubs his chin. The light turns green. "A young man was murdered around there two nights ago. They were mourners on their way to the old cemetery at the end of the street."

"Oh." I want to believe him. I want to believe I'm just imagining things again.

Detective Harris pulls onto Fifth Avenue. He's silent, lost in thought, and I don't dare speak again for I fear something terrible and deadly will come from his lips. He's a powerful man, I can sense it. I wonder if he's ever killed anyone. If he has, I wonder if it haunts him.

Time moves slowly as windshield wipers tick back and forth. His car radio is tuned to a sports channel but the volume is low. I'm able to make out most of what the announcer says, some grave prediction on the outcome of an NFL Wild Card game airing later tonight.

Harris glances at me. "You like football?

Warm memories of my father standing on the sidelines and snapping photographs flood my head. "My Dad was a sports photographer for the *Providence Journal*," I tell him, my voice again my own. "He used to take Allie and me to the games sometimes when we were kids." I wonder what's happened to my father's collection of photographs, all the negatives he once had so meticulously cataloged and tucked away in plastic sleeves. Did Allie sell them, or did she simply abandon them? She always just walked away from things, never looking back and seldom concerned with who or what she left behind.

"That must be where you got your talent from, your father." The detective turns onto Broadway, leans over to turn the radio lower. "You still follow the game?"

"I did for a while, even after my Dad got killed." That was ages ago, a time when Dad, Allie and I would drive to Schaefer Stadium in weather like this to watch the Patriots play. It felt safe then—even if the highway was sheer ice, even if we were in the middle of a nor'easter—it seemed nothing could harm us. Until the night our car skidded on black ice, veered off the highway and flipped over. From that night forward, I no longer had the luxury of little girl dreams of safety and warmth.

My father hadn't believed in seatbelts. He was thrown through the windshield and killed instantly. I escaped with whiplash, Allie with cuts on her face and a few bumps and bruises. We survived, but were never the same.

I want those days back so badly. Our father never should have died that way.

I saw the demons that night, sitting up high in stadium bleachers just hours before the accident happened. Later, they hovered over the crashed car, trying to capture my father's spirit as it spiraled from his dead body. But he was too good, too pure for them.

I know he's someplace safe now.

"I remember you telling me about the accident." The detective's voice, now softer, interrupts my memories, but gently. He seems to sense my sorrow. It must be more evident than I realize. "But you never mentioned your mother."

"She left us when we were little," I tell him. "We could fend for ourselves by the time we lost our father." I close my eyes and see her flailing her hands like a mad woman, telling me I'd see the demons one day. "I don't even know if the bitch is dead or alive."

The detective shakes his head. His ring glistens as a light turns from red to green. "So, Allie came to New York to be with you?"

How many times has he asked me the same question? My answer is always the same. "I came here first, she followed. Whether it was to be with me, I'm not sure. That was part of it, but…" I remember Allie showing up at my door, a suitcase in one hand, a half smoked joint in the other. She told me she was running from her boyfriend Ronnie, because he had abused her. There were dark blue bruises around her eyes and her lips were cut and swollen. She looked so scared. "Her boyfriend beat her," I said. "She came here to get away from him."

Harris nods. He knows the story. I've repeated it countless times. "The guy who did it, Ronnie Bateman, was murdered the day your sister left."

"I didn't know." He's probably better off dead. My sister's face flashes before me. She loved the son-of-a-bitch, hooked up with him in junior high and took his shit for years. He was good looking, wild and mean. Dad wouldn't allow him to come to the house, but he knew how Allie felt about Ronnie. He knew he couldn't do anything about who his daughter fell in love with. "How long have you known about Ronnie? Why didn't—"

He seems to be driving in circles. Didn't we pass this block before? "I wanted to make sure Allie was in the clear. I didn't want to lay more bad shit on you, that's all."

"Allie wouldn't kill anyone. She was irresponsible, not a murderer." I hear my voice crack.

"I know that, Gina." He bites his lower lip as if lost in thought for a moment. "But I want you to get something through your head. She's not in that church. There's nothing for you there."

"I don't know how—"

"Keep away from there," he says, waving a hand to silence me. "There are beliefs and places in this city that are incomprehensible to some—Hell—to *most*, and it's best to leave them alone." He unlocks my door. "I'll call you if I hear anything."

I watch him a moment then open the door and step onto the

walk without a word. Snow stings my eyes, and I swing the door closed.

The detective drives away. Shadows waver around his vehicle, and faces leer from the back window. I know Harris can't see them; even in a crowd, they only haunt the lonely.

There are beliefs and places in this city that are incomprehensible to some—Hell—to most, and it's best to leave them alone.

I wonder if Harris is a good lover. I could have asked him if he wanted to come up, if he needed a hot drink, but he's probably got a wife and kids. I've been with married men before, and after a while you want more, you want to walk out in the open. You want to tell people how good they are in bed, but you keep the secret in your gut until you can't take it anymore. Then you end it before it destroys you.

I remove keys from my pocket and make my way to the door, my mind working various scenarios. If Tony's home, I could tell him to leave, but I should wait until the storm is over. He'd end up sleeping in the park or in an alley. People die in weather like this.

I'll give him warmth, save him from all that…for now.

6

The super, a middle-aged man named Frankie Madero, stands in the hallway, shovel in hand. His eyes are watery and his beefy face is redder than usual. He's gained weight, and his massive belly hangs over his belt. His jacket is fastened with a series of safety pins because he can no longer close the snaps comfortably over his massive torso. I wonder if he was once handsome, if some time long ago he had passion for something or for someone unobtainable. I wonder if he gave up on his dreams, or if he ever had any at all. I think everyone starts out with dreams, but people tell themselves there's no time, not enough money, it's too difficult, they're too old, or it's not meant to be. People murder their dreams without even bothering to give them proper burials. People laugh when they remember things they once believed they could have, and call themselves fools for ever believing they could. Do you go to Hell because you've given up on your dreams? Or does life on Earth become the hell?

Frankie smiles when he sees me. "I'm surprised you were out in this. Ain't no day for farting around in the city." He moves toward the door. "I'll shovel what's out there. Better to do a bit now. If I wait 'til the storm's done then it'll be too high, too heavy."

He's not wearing gloves and his clothing is thin. His jacket is worn at the elbows and the pockets are torn. Is his paycheck so small that simple needs go unfulfilled? "Be careful, Frankie, it's freezing out here."

"Yep." He lifts the shovel. Thick dark liquid trickles from the edges. I notice the same rusty red stains on his jeans.

I watch him disappear into swirling clouds of white and wonder if he gave up another identity to live in his little shoebox dwelling, if he once killed someone in another state, perhaps another borough.

Perhaps he's eluded police with his disguise. Maybe he still has the murder weapon and brings it out when it storms. He knows no one will see him through all the ice and snow.

Imagination can be a demon. It can terrify, make you want to bolt your doors on a clear sunny day when others are enjoying life, loving each other without apology or compromise. A painted devil, it torments and drives lovers and friends away. Uncontrolled, it can make you insane.

The super isn't bright or clever enough to elude the police. He's a simple man living a simple life. For some reason, this makes me smile. If I didn't know better I might even envy him.

The door to his small room just off the front hall is open. Something inside smells good, so I take a quick peek. His companion, a younger woman named Lilly, thin with wild eyes and brittle hair, is stirring something in a large pot on the stove. Smoke curls around her as she hums and taps her foot. She sinks her fingers into a small copper bowl to her right, sprinkles ingredients into the bubbling pot then looks up and sees me standing here. She gives a wide smile. "I put love potion in Frankie's stew, keeps him from straying. Got to do what you need to, ya know?" She begins to stir quickly, laughing at a joke only she understands.

At least Frankie has someone to love. Love can get you through a lot of shit, and maybe true love is all he ever wanted, all he ever dreamed of.

I wish I had real love.

I climb the stairs, dreading the emptiness waiting for me inside my apartment. A dull ache emerges from my heart as I think of Tony. Again, I find myself wondering where he is and why he's been lying to me. I approach my door, fumble for my keys in my purse and absently touch the knob. The door is open, but Tony isn't here. If he was, his boots would be drying in the hall and his portable easel would be leaned against the banister. Did I forget to lock up? Or has someone broken in? Maybe a madman is sitting on my living room couch, drinking my wine and waiting for me. He could strangle me with his bare hands, or with the belt from my robe.

Someone abducted my sister and killed her. Detective Harris said he may have been watching her, tracking her every move. I figured he'd come for me sooner or later.

I step gingerly inside the apartment and quickly flick on the light.

The couch is empty but for a pair of Tony's sweats and some bread crumbs scattered haphazardly across it.

I slip a can of pepper spray out of my purse, clip it to my belt and then lower my purse to the floor.

I walk to the bedroom. Everything is as I left it. The bed is unmade, shades are drawn and the rug still needs to be vacuumed. Tony's abstract paintings hang above the bed and bureau. I throw open the closet door. It smells of mothballs. Fake furs and sequined clothes are draped over paint-splattered denim. Our jeans, sweaters and cotton shirts are mixed together. It's a tangled mess. I should straighten it out soon. I look to the floor. An assortment of sneakers, boots and summer sandals are there. I gaze at a beaded black satin pump. Its mate is missing, has been for months. I wonder if the killer broke in here and stole it, if he holds it, strokes it like a lover and thinks about a day when he'll kill me. I loved that fucking pair of shoes. How dare a maniac deprive me of such a simple pleasure? I carefully part clothing, hold my breath in anticipation of an ax murderer leaping out at me. But no one is there. Maybe I've watched too many cop shows on TV, read way too much noir and am simply overreacting. I wonder if my sister thought the same things before she was killed.

Pushing those thoughts aside, I crouch down, peek beneath the bed. Nothing but dust balls and several mismatched socks.

I walk down the small hallway, peer into Tony's small studio but find only canvases and easels. Off to the side is my darkroom. A killer hides there. I know it. I push open the door. Smells of photographic chemicals greet me. Photographs are pinned to wire across the small room. I open cabinets beneath the sink, above my enlarger. No one hides. Only basins and supplies are there. I cross the hallway and enter the kitchen. Dishes are still in the sink and the table is cluttered with books and newspapers. I enter the bathroom and pull open the shower curtain to reveal white porcelain and a shampoo bottle.

I simply must have forgotten to lock the door...but where the fuck is my black satin shoe?

I walk back to the living room.

Exhausted, I strip off my clothes and lay on the couch. My muscles ache and my hands and knees sting from the fall. I'll sleep, I promise myself, and wait for Tony's return. Snow sticks to the windows as the wind beyond them howls. I hear Frankie and his girlfriend laughing downstairs. I can't make out precisely what they're saying, but I hear a word now and then. *"Sister...Allie... dead."* There's another voice, somber, low. It sounds like Detective Harris, but that's unlikely.

All the voices join in a lulling chorus. *"Suspicious...can't be sure... watching."*

Afraid the dreams may be starting again, I open my eyes, resist sleep. It won't be long until Tony gets back from wherever the fuck he is—I'll sleep then.

A neighbor's cat cries, and I think of an old cat I had as a child. Her name was Martha, and she used to cuddle close to me at night. I'd wake up if she wandered away to a windowsill or to a comfortable chair, and I'd be afraid because then the voices would come and shadows would spiral from beneath the closet door. I'd call her back to bed and she'd come, leap up next to me and nuzzle close like a protective mother.

"Sister."

It's not Allie's voice...it's no one's voice I know. It's evil and shrill.

"Martha," I say softly. Something soft and warm is near and despite it all my eyes close and I feel myself drifting off to sleep as snow covers the city.

I dream of an old bookstore where Shakespeare's manuscripts are for sale along with my photographic stories of Manhattan. There's a vintage clothing store next door. As I scan racks of clothing a woman and child approach me. The woman says, "You're ancient, but you look young. Reminds me of vampirism."

I get a creepy feeling, but smirk at her and say, "Yeah, great. Thanks."

Next, I dream Tony and I are laughing, making love, and I tell him I want to make it work. He says he'll change and I believe him. I tell him we should never give up on our dreams. He tells me I'm ancient, that the blood I need is at the church in Harlem. We hug, and we're happy despite the eerie feeling in my gut.

"We've got to make it work," I say as my eyes slowly open. "This dream won't die."

The wind howls louder, and I drift back to sleep, thinking about things I need to tell Tony when he gets back.

7

The dead of night, everything's still and covered with the fog of sleep. Tony's tattered army jacket is gone from its spot where it hangs next to the door, and I don't sense him in the bedroom. I always feel his presence when he's near. I shouldn't care where he is or who he's with, yet I long for him, want him back. Instead, I'm all alone. Not even the dark things are with me tonight. They must be haunting others.

The apartment is cold, but we can't afford to keep the heat up high. Oil heat is too expensive and the electric heaters we used last month just spiked our electric bill. Money's tight, even with me working. I got in over my head with some credit cards, paying for Tony's art supplies and spending at downtown shops like there's no tomorrow. Then there's my addiction to eBay and my inability to resist rare occult books bound in leather. My bookshelves are crammed with volumes about mysticism, time travel and devil worship. I haven't read any of them, I just admire the way they look stacked against each other. I dust them daily, savor their old smells and dream about the secrets within their pages. Maybe one day I'll learn them. My only usable credit card went over its limit with my last purchase; a publication documenting voodoo rituals using human sacrifice. I think of the old church in Harlem. The dead were given to strange and obscure Gods in exchange for power, money or twisted love.

The CD player comes on and Billie Holiday's sultry voice fills the apartment. Her man left her. I hear Tony singing along. Did he come in while my thoughts drifted, as sleep came and went? I notice his coat hanging in its usual spot now, where it should be, the edges dripping with water, making little circular puddles on the floor. He always sings when he's drunk. I rise, rub my eyes and make my way to the music, to Tony, but he's not here. The room is empty.

"What the fuck?" I mutter aloud, my voice hoarse.

The ancient elevator creaks. Did Frankie fix it? Footsteps sound.

I run to the door and throw it open, but no one's there. The scent of lemon perfume hangs in the air, reminding me of Allie.

"Sis?" Allie's voice echoes from the stairwell, from darkness, from places where the dead exist.

"Not tonight," I tell the darkness, certain this must be a nightmare. "I can't—I can't handle this tonight." I'm so fucking cold. I gaze into the empty hallway.

A woman moans in the next apartment, but no one lives there. Liquor bottles are piled against a forsaken coat rack in the hallway.

Footsteps sound on the stairs. A figure shrouded in shadow trudges upward, hunched over, hands elongated, torso unnatural.

It must be the way the moonlight slices through storm clouds, casting odd shadows on the stairwell, because Tony appears in the hallway, face flushed, hair wet, coat dripping with newly fallen snow.

He doesn't say a word, just pushes past me, makes his way into the apartment and collapses on the bed. His eyes are watery, and he's shivering. "Shit, it's colder in here than it is out there."

"Money's tight, you know that." I shrug. I don't care. I miss him, need him. "I'm glad you're back. I missed you."

"Come lay down beside me, babe, warm me up." His eyes are glassed over and he smells of old sweat. His hair shimmers with snow droplets.

I glance out the window. The world is dark, nothing visible but for a ghostly light from an apartment across the way and the moon making odd patterns on the walls and floor. When did it get so bad out?

Finally, I lay down beside him. "Missed you." His voice is husky, sleepy.

The volume on the stereo suddenly rises, blasting Billie's voice, deep and sad, through the apartment.

"What the hell's going on?" Tony sits up.

"The stereo's old," I tell him. "It's been coming on and off by itself lately, or getting louder and softer. At first, I thought you were back, but then I remembered the fucking thing's haunted. Who cares? Don't you just love her voice?" I kiss his cheek.

"I'm in the mood for rock." Tony turns over on his side. "I'm so tired, though."

"I came to see you today. You weren't on West Broadway. They said you haven't been there in a while." I close my eyes, certain I don't really want to know where he's been and wondering even then why I'm asking.

"I moved my stand up to the 80s, more business there—will be when the weather breaks anyway. This guy I know, Al, he lets me put my stuff under the awning of his pizza shop. He says I can attract business and we can both make out." His voice is flat and devoid of emotion, the way it always is when he lies to me.

"I should try harder to sell my stuff," I say. "Maybe I should put a stand next to yours."

"It's tough there. Wait until spring." Tony sighs, shuts off the light.

Clouds are now moving past the moon. I can't see him anymore. The door clicks shut, footsteps shuffle in the hall, and the elevator makes a grinding noise. I wonder if I've drifted off to sleep without realizing it and am coming to just then, because as I move my hands over the mattress I realize Tony is gone again.

I pull myself up, get out of bed and pad to the living room. I look out the window into the alley and see him down there leaning against his van. He appears to be in deep conversation with a girl shrouded in an old fur coat, her head covered with a dark scarf.

"Allie was dressed like that before she disappeared," I hear myself say. "She borrowed my coat and scarf." I feel nauseous and suddenly lightheaded. "What—what's happening down there?"

"What? Man, you tripping or what?" Tony's says from somewhere behind me.

I spin on my heels, see Tony lying on the bed, eyes brown and drowsy.

I don't remember coming back in here. I don't remember waking from a dream.

Snow batters the windows as I move past the bed to my dresser. I open the middle drawer, see the newspaper clippings yellowed and dog-eared that lay in neat piles there, where I keep them, where

I've kept them since this all began.

Sacrificial Murders in Harlem, the headlines read, *Young Woman Missing*.

I slam shut the drawer, lie on the bed and close my eyes. Tony touches me, kisses me and talks in his sweet and sexy voice. "It's all right, what you did is all right. It all comes back around, fucking shit doesn't stop, you know."

"I'm glad you came back," I tell him.

"I'll never leave you. Some things are forever." I swear I see the demon man staring back at me for a moment, but when headlights drift by and set the dark of night on fire I realize it's Tony—only Tony—looking back at me.

I wrap my arms around him, listen to the storm and allow darkness and his flesh to consume me. At that very moment, I don't care about anything else.

I just want to forget and make love to my man.

8

L oneliness is a bitch on Sundays.

Tony rises before dawn, gathers his paintings and leaves me here alone. He used to wake me and we'd have breakfast and talk. We used to take our time making love. Now everything is rushed. Things have been dreary, and obviously something's wrong. This morning is no different, Tony didn't bother to let me know his day had begun and he was gone by the time I woke up. He didn't leave a note and I know he won't call later. This shouldn't surprise me, of course, since he's never committed to anyone and has always been a vagabond artist, loving paint and canvas more than flesh and blood or the warmth of a woman. What made me think I could change him?

I think about Detective Harris. Does he make slow love to his woman on Sunday mornings, or does he rush off into predawn thinking about murderers, thinking about how he can save the city from the decay of twisted, unspeakable acts? Can he love a woman more than the stirrings of his soul? Does he seek warmth from carnal knowledge, or is it merely a way to relieve the stress of his life? I shouldn't think about him. I've got to set things straight with Tony before I do that.

Tony. He was warm last night, almost loving, but maybe it was a dream. It still seems surreal, like time was moving back and forth, mixing up events, and making things off balance. Maybe I should find another doctor, get some medication that clears my head. I won't go back to the last one. I won't listen to her talking trash about my mother. I need somebody who'll help me.

Someone please help me.

I stand at the window, hold a cup of steaming coffee and gaze into the alley. Children play down there, bundled in warm coats, gloves and hats. Smoky cold air streams from their lips when they laugh, and it reminds me of Allie and me playing in the snow. Those winters in Boston were the best of our lives, so innocent and happy. Dad always made sure we were warm and that we went back in the house before dark, and Mom would just watch from her window, every now and then cocking her head to the side as though she heard someone speaking. I'd gaze up at her staring down from a second-floor window. Her face was solemn and her eyes had a faraway look, as though she looked beyond Allie and me to things no one else could. Maybe my old doctor was right. Maybe there was something terribly wrong with my mother, but I don't want to remember her that way. I refuse to. Maybe I'm too much like her.

Someone knocks at the door. I figure it's probably Frankie, since the rent's late. It was due last Tuesday but I needed to stall until I got paid on Friday.

Another knock.

"Coming." I grab my purse, open the door.

Detective Harris, not Frankie, smiles down at me. "Got a few minutes, Gina?"

"Yeah, come on in."

He's wearing blue jeans and a black leather jacket. He slips leather gloves off, shoves them in his coat pocket then rubs his hands together. His ring catches the light. The engraved serpent seems to wriggle. "Cold out there. I smell coffee. Is it still hot? You know, on second thought tea would be better—if you have it. I've had way too much coffee today already."

"Sure. Follow me." I throw my purse down on the couch, lead him into the kitchen then motion for him to sit. I pour hot water from a kettle on the stove into a ceramic mug and grab a teabag from the canister. "Sugar and cream?"

"No, this is fine." He picks up the cup, closes his eyes as he drinks. He sips, seems to savor the taste a moment then sets the cup down. "Tastes good, thanks."

"I've got some donuts. Cinnamon—"

"No, I don't need the carbs. Sit down, Gina." He's silent, as if gathering his thoughts and won't speak until it's all perfect in his head. My father was the same, always thinking ahead, always careful with his words, a stone statue frozen in time, chin resting on his hand, forever contemplating questions an ancient sculptor chiseled into his head. But the detective is here for a reason. Cops don't just drop by unless they've got questions. I wait for him to speak, and after a few minutes, his words take shape. He removes a grainy photograph from his pocket. "You know this guy?"

I smile. A young black man with a crooked smile, braided hair and a small scar over his left eye looks into the camera. "That's Rico. He hustles knockoff bags down on Canal. Allie and I used to get fake Gucci's and Louis Vuitton's off him." My heartbeat quickens. I look Detective Harris in the eye. "I can't get in trouble for it, can I?" I think of how Allie went much further than that.

"We don't generally arrest people for buying knockoffs," he says with a hint of sarcasm, "and we only pinch the vendors when there's nothing else going on. Even then, that's not exactly my department." His eyes turn intense and he points to the photograph. "Back to your buddy, Rico. We suspect he may have taken his hustle a bit further."

"How much further?"

"He doesn't hustle on street corners anymore. Now he keeps his stash in an empty office building a few blocks over from Canal, tempting chicks with Coach's, Vuitton's, Gucci's—you name it." He bites his bottom lip. "We found a body in a dumpster outside his building, young girl. She had a fake Gucci slung over one arm, and an inverted cross was carved into her chest. Other shit I can't get into."

"Bodies turn up in the city all the time."

"We searched every office in that building. Most were empty or occupied by struggling, but legitimate businesses. All except for Rico's so-called office. Lots of suspicion there, but that's all it is for now. We shut down his counterfeit operation. Normally we'd look the other way." He stops speaking for a moment. I know there's more to what they found in that office—near that body—but he can't tell me. He thinks for a moment and then begins to speak again. "We held Rico a day for illegal vending, but we don't have enough evidence to tie him to the murder. Forensics couldn't tie his DNA to the body, couldn't prove the girl had been up to his place. The knockoff bag and carving proved to be circumstantial. We cut him loose first thing this morning."

"Why are you telling me all this?" I ask.

He sips tea and then says, "Did he ever say anything or do anything to scare you or your sister?"

"Rico? No, he's always been sweet. I know he hustled with a couple Asians guys and some dude from the Caribbean. I didn't really know them, though, maybe you should talk to them."

"We questioned the Asians and the guy from the islands. They're on our list, but Rico's the main suspect right now. Did he ever mention being in an offbeat religion, ritualistic shit?"

"No, never."

I can see Rico moving up close to women when they walk down Canal. He's saying, "*Coach, Prada, Louis Vuitton…*" He talks low, slow and seductive like he's inviting a chick to bed, like he's talking dirty to her. I shake my head. "Rico wouldn't hurt anyone, believe me."

"That's the problem. Girls like you and your sister are too trusting. Can't be in this city." Harris touches my hand.

"Tell me more about Allie. Would she have gotten involved in stuff like that?"

"Hustling knockoff bags or ritualistic murder?"

He stares at me, apparently not finding my attempt at humor amusing.

"Look, Allie was weird," I tell him. "Sometimes she did bizarre things just for the hell of it. She had a strange outlook on life. I know for a time she stood on the corner of West Houston and hustled purses for Rico. She did it for a kick, once for a wine-colored Prada he'd promised her. There were other things—she'd get obsessed and do weird shit."

"Like what?"

"We used to take the Metro to New Haven on Saturdays sometimes, go to basketball games at the Coliseum. There was this guy who collected our tickets—nice looking, Spanish—she used to flirt with him, go have a smoke with him out on the platform when the train stopped in New Rochelle. They weren't supposed to, but they did. She started riding the Metro every Saturday, back from Grand Central to New Haven, just to see him—just to smoke with him. I'm not sure if anything else went down between them." I remember hickeys on her neck once when she came back from riding the Metro, and another instance when her blouse had blood stains on it. *Merely circumstantial,* as the detective would say. I don't mention it.

"Odd." Detective Harris smiles. "But attraction makes you do strange things at times." His hand is still on mine.

"It stopped after a couple months. She told me one day he just wasn't there anymore." I sigh, remember riding that train before Allie started going without me, looking out the window on the way back from basketball games and how it was so dark and some places were so desolate I thought I'd seen demons looking back. I wonder if those demons took the guy away one night when he was standing out there smoking. I wonder if Allie called them.

"Gina, people get transferred. They quit, get fired." Detective Harris moves his hand away from mine.

"They die."

"I know it sucks, I know you're feeling all kinds of guilt and fear, but let's be real here, OK?"

I think of something to say, anything to keep his eyes from boring into mine. "You said you were watching people. Who else do you suspect?"

"Look, I've told you a lot already."

"Ok, sure."

"The city's strange." He sips tea, smiles at me. "Lots of things happen that can't be explained. This city has history and lots of people are intertwined in that history. They've left a legacy of death and horror. I know a lot—too much about obsession—about how religion is perverted." He stops speaking and sighs.

Has he seen the things I've seen? Does he know what Allie saw?

"Thanks for the tea." Detective Harris looks at his watch then stands. "We're still watching Rico, but if you remember anything or anyone else, call me."

"I will." I think of the black woman. Why am I dreaming of her? Why did she speak to me yesterday? The detective looks at me as if he knows what I'm thinking.

"Don't keep anything from us, even if it might seem...*strange.* Hell, even dreams can hold secrets." He hesitates a moment. "I've seen a lot of craziness, a lot of things that defy reality. You're not alone, Gina."

I understand. I'll tell him more, one day, but not now. "Goodbye, Detective."

"It's Daniel, call me that, OK?" He turns to go.

I don't follow him, listen instead to his footsteps, to the sound of the door squeaking then shutting behind him. I wonder what the hell my sister was into and what this other woman has to do with it. I'm afraid and wish I could run after the detective—after Daniel— and drive away with him through Manhattan on this quiet Sunday morning.

I lock the door and make myself another cup of coffee. I'll stay in today and hide from the danger out there. But I know I still won't feel safe. Not today. Not ever.

9

Daniel's cup remains on the table. The napkin he used is beside it. Tea trickled down the ceramic when he drank, and a small pool of tea and remnants of the bag remain at the bottom. I don't want to wash it, not yet. I want the memory of him to linger a while. It was good talking with him, and I find myself wishing I knew more about him, about his life.

My father always read the newspaper when he drank his morning coffee. He'd make Allie and me eggs and bacon on Sunday mornings along with fresh-squeezed orange juice. My mother would sit there with a cigarette dangling from her lips, the ashes falling in her plate, her eyes empty and void of emotion. One Sunday morning Allie, only eight at the time, turned to me and whispered; "The demons got Mommy. They told me last night."

"No such thing, Allie," I said with the ten years of wisdom I'd felt I'd acquired. "Daddy says Mommy's just stressed. Her last job gave her nerves. That's all."

"It's the demons. They're all around her. Can't you see them?" She pursed her lips. "One of them hit Matthew McDrake when nobody was looking."

Earlier that week Matthew McDrake, a first-grader, had emerged from the school playground, nose bloody, right eye swollen and black. When teachers asked him who'd hurt him he merely repeated over and over, "A scary-looking guy dressed in old-fashioned clothes."

"No way, Allie, it was some drunk guy who wandered down from the projects. Police are looking for him."

Allie put her folk down carefully. "It was a demon." Her little girl eyes seemed wise beyond their years. "Kids, eat your breakfast.

Stop with the secrets." My father's eyes twinkled. I'm sure he thought we were sharing innocent childhood chatter. Maybe we were, maybe not.

Even as a child Allie seemed devoid of innocence. She was a strange and precocious child, a loner who chose to devour the works of Emily Dickinson, Sylvia Plath and other dark, innovative poets, in favor of dolls and childhood games. She drew pictures of sinewy, hooded creatures she claimed she dreamed about. The nightly news and adult crime shows captivated her. She knew Santa did not exist long before I did. She grew into a pretty teenager, and then a beautiful, intelligent young woman, running with people from offbeat and dark subcultures. She wore dark clothing, dyed her chestnut hair black and wrote Goth poetry which was often published in rags run by people who claimed to drink blood. Rather than the hippest nightspots in town, she could more often be found frequenting local graveyards. "It's the core of our being," she once told me while painting her nails blood red. "We come from darkness. Our souls are sick and we're reborn again and again in hopes of redeeming ourselves. Most of us fail, so why not embrace the evil, the demons that surround us?"

For a while she painted with a fervor she'd generally reserved for passionate affairs or wild spending sprees. It was the summer she fell in love with an art professor from the city college. She created at least three canvases a week, brilliant abstract pieces in black, deep reds and slashes of pure white. I still have one of her paintings. It hangs above a bookcase in the living room. I find it profound amidst Tony's lesser work. In the painting, cathedrals and skeletal trees are strewn here and there. A winged figure flies above the bleak landscape, blood spurting from its head as its finger touches a cross atop a towering spire. I am always reminded of death when I look closely at it, and sometimes I'd swear I can hear Allie's demons speaking to me.

Did you go away with them, Allie? Is that why they never found your body? Are they coming for me now too?

Time has passed way too quickly. It's getting late, almost dark now. A shadow seems to swiftly pass over me. I used to feel safe here, but not anymore, like they're breaking through.

Something thuds outside my door. I hear Frankie talking in

the hall. There's a man with him, but I can't make out the voice. I walk to the door, press my ear up against it and listen. It's not Dave Sousa, a co-worker of mine who lives in the building, or any of the men who live on the block. They're moving away, heading down the stairs. Words are muddled, meaningless and slurred by liquor.

"Cops—trouble—ain't got patience for this—" Frankie laughs once, as though pausing to take another swig from a bottle of beer.

The other voice is sarcastic, malicious. "Bitch is gonna go down."

I know that voice. I close my eyes and see a man with clothes from another time. Loud laughter breaks out. Another thud sounds. It repeats over and over. Something—someone—has fallen down the stairs. Frankie in a drunken stupor? Laughter sounds again.

The front door opens and closes and then everything's quiet.

I open my apartment door a crack. There's a streak of blood stretching from here to the top of the stairs. I click the door shut, lock it behind me.

Footsteps sound up the stairs. A key turns in the latch and the door slowly opens.

I scream.

"What the fuck is wrong with you?" Tony's standing there. He seems to be mocking me.

"I heard something, thought somebody…"

He waves his hand. "You need a drink. You spend too much time locked up in this hole." His face is flush from the cold. "I'm hungry. Let's go for a slice and get a glass of wine. Get your coat, come on."

"OK." I tell myself it'll be all right. I'm going out with my man and there are no demons, there's no danger out there. It'll be just Tony and me walking in the snow, talking like lovers do and being normal. It'll be a good night.

10

It's beautiful walking through Downtown when snow is falling. Store owners have shoveled walks, and cars creep by slowly. The moon is a crescent, shining amidst winter stars, a magical sliver of light above the snow-covered city. I'm reminded of an old book I once bought from a vendor simply called The Moon. The front cover is signed by its previous owners, six in all. It was new in 1921. Now the spine is cracked and the cover stained. I often wonder about its previous owners. Were they into magic, Astrology? Were they kind or wicked? Do their spirits live on within brittle pages?

A book vendor packs up his wares as we cross onto East Houston. I wonder if he has treasures there, if there are relics about the moon—about magic. I want to stop, but he looks cold and in a hurry to get into his nearby van. I don't mind the cold. Tony holds me close, singing an old jazz tune I've heard in my dreams.

His boots crunch on the icy walk and snow glimmers on his dark hair. He's a prince from a childhood fairytale, dark and sweet. Nothing can harm me. Creatures do not tower above on city rooftops, wicked sounds do not emanate from alleys. "Turn here," Tony says as we approach a corner restaurant with red, white and green neon announcing Angelo's Pizzeria. "Good food, just opened." He ushers me inside and to the bar. A few people are there. A middle-aged man drinks his beer and studies a racing form. He scratches his chin and makes marks on the form with a Sharpie. A woman, overweight, with blonde frizzled hair sucks on a cigarette, dollar bills are spread out in front of her. Her blouse is low cut, her skirt too short. She smiles. I notice bright red lipstick smeared on her front teeth. She's flirting with the bartender, winking when he passes by her, reaching out to touch his hand. He's young, walks with an air of arrogance. His repulsion towards the woman is noticeable. New York is filled with sad and lonely people, with those who beg for a moment of attention, who'll pay for an hour of love. They die alone, their plots unattended, forgotten and swallowed up by a city that preys on them. It takes away their youth, dims hopes once bright.

Do fallen angels reside here? I wonder. Do they walk among us, seeking the weak, and do they lure them toward demise, reduce them to sacrifices for this city of light, this city of dark?

Some days I think I've seen them. Some days I know I have.

A man sits at the end of the bar in shadow. I cannot see his face, but I can see he's dressed in an old suit jacket and that his white shirt has a vintage look to it. He's holding a cigarette and thick clouds of smoke swirl around him. I know him. I'm happy now. He'll stay in shadow as long as I remain so. The smoky veil will keep him separate from my world tonight.

"It smells great in here. I'm so hungry." I slide onto a barstool. "They serve food at the bar?"

"Yeah, we can get a slice here." Tony looks toward the man. It seems as though he's receded further into darkness. The bartender smiles at me. "Beer?"

Tony turns to me. "You ought to try the cheese and veggie pizza. It's to die for, but if you want something else…"

"OK then, two beers and two slices of cheese and veggie pizza. And two large salads-the Italian kind with hot peppers and stuff." I pluck a black sequined wallet from my shoulder bag, noticing a puzzled look on the bartender's face.

"Sure." The bartender motions for a waitress to take our order. She looks at me, sizes me up, shakes her head and moves toward the dining area.

Tony kisses my cheek. "Going to the little boy's room, be back in a sec."

"OK." I watch him make his way to the end of the bar. He disappears in darkness and smoke, and I see the orange tip of a cigarette glow, a skeletal hand extending from shadow. Low and menacing laughter, barely audible, trickles from the dark end of the bar.

I listen to chatter from the dining area, watch people come and go. A small child cries and a siren sounds outside. I gaze at my watch. Tony's been gone for ten minutes. A blast of cold air fills the bar and a door clicks shut. Someone touches my shoulder. I turn. Rico stands there. He looks frightened. Beads of sweat are on his forehead. "Gina, we gotta talk, man."

"I'm with my boyfriend. Can it wait—I mean—"

"You meeting him? Didn't see anyone with you when you came in." Rico looks to the end of the bar. The man leans forward. His eyes are cold, black, inhuman. "No, Tony just went to the bathroom."

"Twenty-five bucks and thirty-two cents." The bartender slaps down two beers, two slices of pizza and two huge salads.

I give him a twenty and a ten. "You're all set."

The bartender notices Rico and smiles. "Enjoy."

A figure—something—slithers past us. It moves like an aged sullen spirit. I smell Tony's cologne. I hear his laughter. A chill fills the bar and I'm compelled to look to the doorway. Tony moves through it, shoulders slumped, hands tucked deep inside his pockets. He's sneaking away. A woman wearing a sequined shawl is in front of him. It looks as though her boots do not touch the pavement. She remains in front of him, ethereal and somewhat sinister. They both float away, thieves who have robbed me of tonight's happiness.

Fucking Tony. Who did he pick up while he sauntered towards the restroom? Has he gotten into trouble? The woman he left with was wearing a shawl like Allie's. This is crazy. They may not have even been together. Maybe he got a call, had to split. He'll explain later. No matter. It's nothing that hasn't happened before.

I notice the man at the end of the bar is gone. What the fuck.

Rico looks puzzled as tears well in my eyes. "Sit down. Have some beer and food." I motion to Rico and he quickly accepts my offer. He is thinner than the last time I saw him. His tough demeanor is gone.

He picks up a beer mug and takes a long drink. He reaches for pizza and within seconds half the slice is devoured. He wipes his mouth with the sleeve of his jacket then he looks at me, embarrassment etched across his face. "Look, I've been sleeping on the street, haven't eaten in a few days. Cops confiscated all my goods. They shut down my operation. I'm in deep shit besides that, man."

I'm not hungry now. I push my salad and pizza towards Rico,

but hold onto my beer. "Eat. Maybe the super of my apartment building will let you sleep in the basement if you help him shovel some snow, clean up around there. He's done it with other guys in the past."

Rico nods. "Thanks. I need to lay low."

I watch and drink my beer as he devours the two salads and pizza. I order another slice and have the bartender wrap it for him. I button my coat, slip on my gloves and gently tug at Rico's elbow. "Come on. We'll go talk to Frankie."

"I need to talk a little to you first, don't want people listening."

"OK. What's up?"

He looks around then leans close to me. I smell old perspiration. His breath reeks of tobacco and something sour. "They found a fucking body outside the building where I was doing business. Fucking chick had her throat cut. They carved shit on her and laid her out like it was a funeral. There were shells and beads all around her, flowers—dead ones—on top of her and an old rosary—with the fucking cross painted red—on her hands."

"Cops told me about the body, but not all the details."

"They found bones—old ones—ones that had been there for a long, long time—under the floorboards in the office I was using. They can't tie any of the shit to me, I had nothing to do with it, I swear, and they know that—but I know they're fucking watching me anyways." His hands shake and tears fill his eyes. "And I know the cops aren't the only ones watching."

"What do you mean?"

Rico trembles. "Look, Allie, your sister, she was into some weird fucking shit. She used to take people up to my place, do shit with them. I mean, at first, I thought it was just for sex, you know, and she didn't want her pickups to know where she lived. So, I gave her a key. We were tight, you know, but after a while it got scary. She left behind all kinds of crap, weird candles, beads, shells. Once she came to the office on a Saturday afternoon, said she had to pee badly. She threw her coat on the floor and made a beeline to the bathroom. Some photographs tumbled out of her pocket. I picked them up one by one and almost screamed. They were of dead people, all cut and fucked up. Don't know where she got them. I shoved most of them back inside her pocket, but I kept one, was gonna show the cops, but after I thought about it I figured they'd incriminate me." He pats a pocket on his coat. "Got it right here. I should bury it, maybe throw it in the Hudson. I keep seeing those people, walking down Canal. Sometimes I-I see them in my fucking dreams."

"Allie couldn't kill anyone," I mumble, unsure if I'm saying it for his benefit or mine.

"The picture's old, looks it anyway." He glances around. "Hey, I don't wanna believe she had anything to do with people dying either, but I got scared. Shit, I told her to quit using my place, I told her, pack up your shells and beads and all the rest of your freaky shit and don't come back. I even had the locks changed. Right after that, she disappeared, and they found that shit down at the church in Harlem."

I feel the fear rising in me now too, but I'm not only scared for myself, but for Tony, for Daniel and for everyone in my life that matters. What happened to Allie? Did they torture her before they killed her? Was her body too mutilated to leave behind and are the pieces scattered all over the city?

I grab Rico's elbow again. "Come on. You can sleep on my couch. I don't care what Tony says. You're not staying alone in some basement."

"Thanks," he says rapidly, "th-thank, thank you. You sure it'll be cool with your boyfriend?"

"Fuck him. Come on."

We make our way out to the street. The snow has intensified even more, falling steady now and making it difficult to walk without feeling chilled to the bone. We put our arms around each other, hold on tight and move through the night to the safety of my apartment. Rico sighs, gazes at the moon and whispers an old prayer I remember from catechism.

I join him, speaking softly so only he can hear, "...deliver us from evil..."

People pass by us, their lips moving in unison with ours. They're all praying. It's a city of frightened people. It's a city of hell.

I hold Rico tighter and he sighs again. We need to talk more. We need to figure out what the fuck Allie was into. We'll have coffee— maybe pick up some wine. We'll sit by the window and comfort each other in so many ways tonight.

11

Rico and I stop to buy some wine at a liquor store on Broadway, two bottles, one white and one red. I know Tony isn't home yet, that he won't be in until late—maybe he won't be back at all—but at the moment all I want to do is sit and talk with Rico, to learn more about what went on with him and my sister. There are so many things I want to ask him, but at first, we only make small talk.

I feel as though we're being watched, as though we're in danger. The streets are empty and eerily silent. It's getting colder and I can feel it seeping into my bones. The snow is heavy and clings to my hair.

A man selling cheap hats and children's windup toys shivers on the corner of Grand and Broadway. "Rico, stop at this stand," I say. "I need a hat." I hate hats, think I look silly in them, but tonight I need one.

The vendor looks tired. His face is smooth, his eyes crystal blue. "I have to go back to Brooklyn. Hate the thought of driving over there in this. Damn city. They hate to pay overtime. The bridge had better be sanded."

I nod at him and quickly pick out a black felt hat, trimmed with sequins. "How much?"

His face softens and he seems less agitated as a snowplow makes its way down Broadway. "Normally ten bucks, but you look cold too. You can have it for six." I give him a ten. He smiles. "Thank you, Miss. God bless." A drift of snow flurries behind him and around him. He's swallowed up by white. I hear him speaking as we move away. "Be safe on this wicked night."

A feeling of warmth spreads through me. It's fleeting, but it's nice to know there are gentle people in this world. Angels standing sentinel while we walk dark pathways. I slip on the hat. The brim is wide and partially covers my view, but I don't care. I think about death, about my sister lying in a grave, hidden, her ghost aching for closure. I wonder if she can feel the chill of this stormy winter night. "Lots of sadness in this world," Rico says as we turn a corner and walk quickly still holding on to each other, the wine bottles and pizza wrapped in brown paper and nestled in his oversized coat pocket. "Lots of scary shit too. There are murderers in this city, crazy people who think nothing of chopping people up." Rico presses closer to me. "I never was afraid to walk these streets." He looks upward. "Something's up there. They're watching us." We pass by an empty office building. Shadows dance behind shaded windows. Rico shakes his head. "Things are getting freaky lately. I see things that I'm not supposed to see…"

"It's happened to me for a while—maybe all my life," I tell him. "I'm not sure of much these days." I pull my hat over my ears as a cold wind sends snow spiraling over the sidewalk. We turn onto East Houston, walk quickly. People stand at crossings waiting for lights to turn. City blocks seem to go on forever. I gaze down Second Avenue. Traffic cruises by, either turning onto East Houston or down Chrystie Street. We walk past Sara D. Roosevelt Park. Lights flank it on each street corner, but deep within strange things seem to hide behind trees, sit on benches, their whispery voices floating through the snow. Cigarette tips glow and boots beat against the earth. A group of leather-clad people emerge, seemingly materializing from shadow.

They step out of the park, walking in single file. They stand in front of us, looking as though they've just emerged from one of the Goth bars in the Bowery, tattooed, pierced and dressed in black from head to toe.

"Evening, got a few bucks to spare?" A man with a buzz cut, a scar on his cheek, a tattoo of a hawk over his left eye leers at us. His fingers are deformed as though his bones have been broken many times, as though they've healed without the help of a doctor. Both his palms have knife wounds and they drip with blood. He must cut himself to feel alive. "Just a couple bucks." Crimson drops fall on white snow.

A woman moves her head back and forth. Her stringy black hair is dry—like death. Her eyes are vacant. She moves to my side, rubs her hand over my coat. "Nice. Can I have it?"

"It's fake." I'm scared, can't think of much else to say.

She laughs at me.

The other man is wearing a hood. It covers his face. "Better still, you got blood to offer us?" The hood slips backwards slightly. White bone and eyes as black as coal are visible. He pulls a knife out of his pocket. "Step into the park, both of you."

"Look, man." Rico takes a step toward them. The hooded man's arm extends forward almost with supernatural speed. Silver gleams. The knife meets Rico's throat.

"Move, you motherfucker." The hooded man leans forward, "Didn't I see you once on a bus going south?" His hood slips back farther and I know these beings are not human. Skull and bone gleam beneath park lights. Corpse fingers grasp the knife's hilt.

A siren sounds. Lights flash.

An unmarked car pulls up on the street beside us.

The door flies open. "Get moving or I'll take you to the tombs." Daniel's voice sounds. He's beside me now. "I mean it. Get going."

I look at the would-be attackers again. They're kids, seemingly alive, stoned and dangerous. Street punks nothing more.

"Move your asses." Daniel's eyes are filled with hate. He looks at bloodstains on snow. He grabs the knife and slips it into his coat pocket.

The hooded guy shrugs. "Just having some fun."

"You hear me, punk? Get lost."

The threesome backs away and recedes into shadow, into a veil of thick snow, back into the depths of Sara D. Roosevelt Park.

Daniel watches them, sighs heavily. "You people OK?"

Rico kicks snow, turns in a circle. "Thank mother of mercy. Thank fucking God and every fucking saint. I never thought I'd be so happy to see you, Detective."

I'm shaking, can't believe all that's gone down tonight. "Yeah, thanks for showing up when you did." I wonder why he's near, why he just happened to show up like this.

Daniel grabs my arm, pulling me away from Rico, who is waving his arms and talking to God, to the stone angels at Saint Patrick's and to the gargoyles at the Dakota.

Daniel's voice is stern, almost fatherly. "I've got my eye on your buddy over there, been watching him all day. Now, may I ask what the hell you're doing with him? He happens to be a suspect in a very—"

"Look," I say, "I've known Rico a long time. He's OK. He just needs a place to crash. He needs a friend."

"Be careful." Daniel smiles, but his eyes are sad. "Call my cell if you need me."

"I will."

"Goodnight." Daniel walks to his car, drives away into a cloud of white snow and smoky streams of exhaust.

Rico is finally standing still. "He hates me."

"He's just being a cop."

Rico looks towards the park. "Those things came straight from Hell."

"They were punks. All we saw were punks, Rico."

"I saw dead things," he insists, pushing me forward. "Don't look back. Just keep walking."

My legs ache and I have a throbbing headache. "Not too much longer."

We approach my apartment building. Frankie's standing on the stairs. His hands are tucked in his pockets and he's shaking his head. "Mrs. Tremaine, lady who lives on the second floor, died this afternoon. Fucking cancer killed her."

Lilly appears, clad only in a light housedress. Mascara is smeared beneath her eyes. She's wearing a sneaker on one foot and a slipper on the other. "Damn disease. She's the fourth person to die on this block from stomach cancer in the past year. Something's in the ground. There's evil shit underneath us and it's going to kill us all." She spins on her heels. "I'm gonna do a spell of protection. I already sprinkled salt all around the building. Coming, Frankie?" He turns and follows her without a word.

Rico and I watch as the lights go on in the hall, and we listen as strange music filters through the door. "Things get weird here sometimes, but Frankie's a good super. The elevator's broke. We have to climb three flights." I want to rush up the stairs, close the door behind me and be safe inside. I'm not afraid of cancer, of toxins and disease seeping up from the ground. I have other things to fear.

"Hurry, it doesn't feel right out here."

We literally run to the door and slam it shut behind us. We laugh nervously as we climb the stairs, clinging to each other until we're safely locked inside my apartment.

Tony's easel isn't in the hall and his coat isn't hanging on the door. I look around. Things are different. "Take off your coat," I say to Rico as I go from room to room. Tony's clothes aren't in the bedroom closet, or in bureau drawers. His canvases aren't in the studio and his whiskey bottle isn't in the wicker basket by the sink. I get drinking glasses out of the cupboard and notice that his oversized coffee mug isn't here. It's as though he never lived with me, as though he was a wish that floated away with the drift of snow tonight.

The hurt is unbearable. He could have told me he wanted to leave. He didn't have to split like this, didn't have to be such a creep about it.

I can hear Rico talking to God, saying a Hail Mary, singing a song from Sunday school.

I walk slowly through the hall. Tony's paintings once hung there and above the bookcase. Now only my sister's painting hangs above my volumes of esoteric books, above secrets written by dreamers who saw beyond the veil of life. Tony had this planned all along. He must have found another chick to live off of, to chisel meals and money from. I tell myself I'm probably better off. It'll hurt for a while, but I'll get by. I always do.

I go back to Rico. He's not praying anymore. There's pizza sauce on his chin. He's holding a bottle of wine, his old coat is on the floor and his shoes beneath the coffee table. "Want to start with the red?" He smiles, but I can tell he's still jittery.

I sit across from him. "Tony's gone, he just split." My voice seems far away, like it's not even me speaking. "Pour me some red."

"Want me to leave? Wanna be alone?"

"Hell, no. Don't go."

Rico looks at his hands. They're shaking a little. His voice is husky. "My boyfriend left too. He woke up one morning and decided he wanted to move to California without me." Rico shakes his head. "It's tough to find somebody you can trust. Not much I can do now."

"We're a forsaken duo, aren't we? At least we're not alone tonight.

At least you're not freezing to death out in the street. Let's get to that wine."

"OK." He opens the bottle. I hand him the glasses and he pops the cork. I watch as red liquid pours from the bottle. He reaches over, places the long-stemmed goblet in my hand.

"Cheers," he whispers to the night, to swirling clouds of white and to our broken hearts.

We drink in silence. One glass and then another. I feel warmth touch the pit of my stomach and then flow through my body. Who are we? Are we people lost and lonely on a snowy night? Adults who are still afraid of the dark, of monsters lurking in shadow? Will we survive? And if not, will it matter to anyone? Will we end up some footnote, a news story, or dead on a sacrificial altar, our hearts sacrificed to the darkness?

I decide to call in sick tomorrow. I haven't done that in months. I need a friend tonight, someone who can help me unravel the mystery of Allie's disappearance, and I know odds are we won't get much sleep. We'll probably talk until the sun comes up. I want to know more about Rico, his past, why a bright and sensitive man ended up hustling knockoff bags on Canal Street. The wine makes me bolder, makes me ask questions I ordinarily wouldn't. "Are your parents in New York? Are they alive?"

"My parents were gypsies, moving from place to place, stealing what they could then running. I think my father hurt people for money, conned the elderly and shit. I think he might have killed somebody. They took him away when we were living in Memphis. Me and my mother came north. She abandoned me when I was ten. I just drifted from foster home to foster home after that. Sometimes I feel like I was born from rot. I mean, sometimes you gotta hustle, gotta hook, gotta steal to get by, but when you have no regard for life, no respect for the weak and vulnerable—not even your own kid—then that's fucking evil." Rico wipes his mouth with his sleeve, looks toward the window. "I'm not stupid. I might have been something if it wasn't for that, you know?" He hangs his head. "I was born from rot. Maybe that's why those things are after me."

I think of my mother, of her screams. Maybe Rico and I are suffering from incurable madness. Maybe it's all that simple, we're just fucking crazy. "You're not a bad person," I tell him. "You can turn your life around."

"Too late for me." He laughs, but it's forced.

"Never too late." I want to believe people can make it despite odds stacked up against them.

"It's way too late. All I know is hustling, dealing. I'll probably end up in a bad place sooner or later. I got no high expectations." He puts his feet up on the table. I don't care. I'm just glad for the company.

"You said something about things we shouldn't be seeing. What did you mean?"

"I was on a bus coming back from somewhere, maybe going somewhere, we were going south I think. I was a kid, wrapped in my mother's arms. My father was asleep in a seat behind us. We were always moving around, like I told you before." He takes a sip of his wine, his eyes turn moist. "I was half-asleep myself. There was a woman, old, frail, sitting across the aisle from us. She was talking about God to the guy sitting next to her, about how this great white light exists high above us, about how we can draw it down, use its power for good."

"Sounds nice."

"Yeah, she said she was coming back from some meeting where all these good people get together from all over the country a few times a year to bring the light down to Earth. She said that other beings are here with us. There are good and bad things, dark and light—but we can't see them, that it has something to do with how fast they vibrate or something. Sometimes the vibration slows and that's when we can see them."

I pour myself more wine, allow Rico to go on uninterrupted.

He stretches then looks toward the window. "Driver stopped somewhere for a pee break. The woman excused herself and walked off that bus with a dozen other people. She stopped at a soda machine and reached into her purse for change. I can still hear the clinking sound when she put her money in the slot. She stopped short. The light on the soda machine was blinking. Poor lady never even pressed the button, to choose either a Coke or an Orange Crush. She stopped short and looked over her shoulder like she heard something and then turned around real slow. Her face was white and her hands started shaking. She was looking at something, mouthing words, but I didn't see anything—or anyone. She was there one minute and the next she wasn't, like she never existed. The other passengers came back and took their seats like everything was normal. The driver just pulled away and nobody fucking said a word, nobody missed her."

"Maybe it was all a dream." I want to believe that Rico's imagination ran away with him, that he was somewhere between a dream and the real world.

"No fucking dream. That guy wearing the hood—I swear—I know it was him sitting beside her on that bus." Rico's voice is somber and he's scaring the shit out of me.

"*Didn't I see you once on a bus going south?*" I see the hooded street punk leaning close to Rico, saying those words. Why would he say that to him unless it was true— unless he was there—on that bus— the night the old woman disappeared?

"It's a nightmare. Tell me it's a nightmare." I drop my glass and it shatters, leaving a red puddle at my feet.

"Why'd they never find Allie's body?" Rico asks me, fear etched across his face. "You ever think about that?"

"I think about it all the time, but she's dead. You don't believe..."

"I'd believe just about anything after all the shit I've been seeing." He reaches into his pocket, pulls out an old wrinkled photograph. "Here's the photo I told you about, one that was in Allie's pocket." He puts it on the table. A beautiful black woman lies on a rose-covered altar. Her dress looks as though it's from the late 1800's or early 1900's. Her hands are folded over her chest. Her throat is cut and it looks as though her heart has been carved out. I've dreamed of her hundreds of times, spoken to her in the street. Rico begins to cry. "I see her all the time, walking down Canal, a ghost, a victim. Now, you tell me what your sister was doing with this fucking picture?"

"I don't know, Rico, but I've seen the woman too. I dream about her."

He folds his arms. "Get another glass. Get a little high, girl."

I go to the kitchen, get a clean glass from the cupboard.

I wonder where Allie's body is, if they did to her what they did to the other woman, or worse. Lights flash outside. I know it's just Daniel watching. I hope he's safe in the night, in the storm. I wonder if Tony is out there somewhere, making love to somebody new. It doesn't matter. I'm not alone. That's all that matters here and now.

12

It's four in the morning. Rico's asleep on the couch, and I sit thinking about angels in the city, the gentle people, the vendors, craftspeople and artists who sell their wares on the street. They are the minority, a subculture that goes unnoticed by those who have reign over this city. Yet they are shining threads within its fabric. Poor souls, but mighty angels amidst the working class who go uptown, downtown and everywhere in between to buy their wares and share early morning greetings. Greetings like prayers to transcendental beings watching and keeping the city from falling off the Earth. Nonetheless they are shunned by the power-driven living for the almighty buck. The rich are the ones who have taken this city hostage. It doesn't matter whether they sit in plush offices on Wall Street or peddle dope to children outside schoolhouses. Greed and self-gratification is their motive. They don't give a damn about the angels who greet you on street corners with invitations to warehouse sales, with sample soaps and bright postcards announcing art shows in DUMBO (down under the Manhattan Bridge overpass) where a new breed of artists reside. Others hang their paintings from wire on the streets of Soho or tend small stands chock full of costume jewelry or handmade leather on Canal. They smile, tell you you're pretty, that you should dress warmer and they touch your hand as though they're spreading magic on your skin. It's often like a dream, walking down Broadway in Soho, through downtown, on Saturday or Sunday—or Times Square during rush hour. People drift in and out of the landscape. I've taken their photographs and sometimes there are halos above their heads. I know it's the sun or a neon light at dusk, but I like to imagine that part of New York must be a slice of Heaven and there are angels there.

Allie loved to shop even more than I do. There were clothes in her closets, in her drawers, with price tags still on them. She'd stack sweaters and jeans in piles on her floor, keep shoes in storage bins under her bed. She had jewelry boxes filled with silver rings and bangle bracelets. It was an obsession, going downtown once a week, and weaving in and out of the shops on Broadway. I don't know how she paid for the stuff. No one would issue her a credit card, not since Chase cut off her Visa, not since her car was repossessed back in Boston. She didn't work steadily either. She served drinks a couple nights a week in a strip joint on Prince Street. Maybe she hooked. I wouldn't put it past her. Bottom line is she could afford the things that were cluttering her apartment.

I cleaned her apartment after she disappeared, put her things in storage. Although I know it's probably just wishful thinking, I still tell myself she might one day come back to claim them. I don't have the heart to take them for myself or to give them away. Months ago, Allie decided to get rid of some of the shit piling up at her place. She called me, asked if I wanted a red leather coat and a couple of mohair sweaters she claimed made her itch. I gladly accepted and told her I'd go by after work. It was a Monday night.

I arrived at my sister's around the same time as her friend Lisa. Allie always suspected Lisa as a closet lesbian, because although she often spoke about men, she rarely dated. She'd flirt a lot but always made excuses as to why she couldn't take things further. Whatever the truth was, she struck me as a sad and insecure soul with virtually no life, hiding from secrets she was afraid to admit even to herself.

That night Lisa stepped into Allie's studio apartment, took off her coat and immediately began telling my sister about a guy she'd just met. "His name is Rich. He just got a job in my building, in the office. We talked last night. I got this vibe off him, you know. I asked around about him. They said he's single." She ran her hand through thick dark hair that always looked a bit greasy and unruly.

Allie smiled slyly at her. "Lisa, go through the clothes I've piled up on the bed. Take whatever you want."

"Thanks!" Lisa's face lit up. "I'm not sure if your stuff fits but I'll try some on."

Lisa chose several pairs of pants and a couple sweaters, put them over her arm and went to Allie's bathroom. Every now and then she'd walk out timidly and ask, "What do you think?" Of course, she'd never look like my sister in those clothes. Lisa was petite, but her waist was thick, her thighs wide and she had almost no bust.

Just the same, Allie would nod each time and say, "Looks cute on you."

Lisa would blush.

My sister turned to me once when Lisa ducked back into the bathroom. "Those clothes, they smell of my perfume, they smell of me. I can imagine her going home and spreading everything on her bed, masturbating with the smells, the textures consuming her."

"You're cold." I smiled when I said it, but Allie's comment bothered me.

What bugged me even more was when Allie grabbed a camera from a shelf and began photographing Lisa each time she put on a new outfit. Lisa began to loosen up, trying clothes on in the open. She looked at my sister as though they were lovers.

"I'm going to make a photo album of you, sweetie," my sister said. Her voice was husky, sexy.

Lisa's face turned bright pink. "Thanks so much for the clothes."

Completely unaware that Allie was making fun of her, Lisa stood there in her underwear, enthusiastically stuffing pairs of pants and sweaters into a shopping bag my sister gave her.

I felt sorry for her but said nothing, did nothing to stop Allie or to protect Lisa.

I wish now I had.

Allie continued to photograph her. Lisa tried to look seductive but it came off as comical.

My sister was being cruel, a tease, and I didn't want any part of it, so I made some excuse as to why I had to leave and took off.

Later that week, I asked Allie what had happened between them after I left.

"Nothing," she told me. "She got dressed and went home. She's way too shy to say what she really wants to. Bet she couldn't wait to do herself, though."

Now I wonder what my sister did with those photos. Were they mixed in with the ones Rico found, with images of dead people? If you attempt to kill someone's soul, isn't it the same, if not worse, than killing their flesh? I suddenly remember the shot I took of the black woman down on Canal and Broadway, and it brings me back to the present. "Shit, my camera." My coat is spread over my legs. I reach into the pocket, remove the digital camera then kick the coat aside. Scrambling over to the desk beside the bookcase, I boot up my computer and slide the memory card into the drive. It was the last shot I took. I click open the file. There's no beautiful black woman in the photo, just a small Asian man holding a necklace, rows of jewelry on hooks behind him.

But Rico said he'd seen her too. "Rico, wake up."

He rubs his eyes, stretches and yawns. "Snow stop?"

"Yeah, a little, but it's bitterly cold now." I bite my lip. "I photographed the black woman, but…" Is she an angel or a demon? Is she part of some sickness I've inherited from my mother? No, Rico saw her too.

"What black woman? I know lots of black women being a black man and all that, you know."

Rico sits up. "We're on the same wavelength here, two people who never quit believing in ghost stories. We're like kids, scared shitless in the dark, afraid of things other people don't think about anymore."

"Yeah, I'm still ten, still hiding under bed sheets with my best friend, still talking about it because I know it's true." This feels natural, as normal as two people discussing photos they've taken of the Brooklyn Bridge beneath a full moon or of the cathedral on Fifth when the sun is setting. "Well, what do you think? I mean, she wasn't there, just the Asian dude and his stash."

"Not sure if she'd photograph that well, being dead and all. Makes sense, there'd be nothing there, no?" He scratches his chin absently. "She just sorta floats down the street. At least she talks to you. She disappears if I take a step towards her—weird—but I'm not afraid of her, not like I should be of a fucking ghost. Anyway, I think you need special film, you know?"

"I guess. I've read books though, sometimes shit like that shows up—like mist—or all blurry—stuff like that." He's right. Shouldn't we be afraid of a dead woman?

"Maybe we're both crazy." He lays down again, closes his eyes. "It's probably my scumbag genes and all the booze and dope. With you it might be grief, plain and simple."

I roll my eyes, but Rico doesn't see. "Never mind. Do you ever think that Heaven and Hell, parts of it anyway, might be right here?"

"What kind of jive you talking to a man who's still drunk and half asleep?"

"Come on, Rico, I'm serious."

"I've always thought that," he says groggily, "ever since that bus trip when I was kid."

"Go back to sleep."

Rico's eyes open and then close. "Night." he's snoring within seconds. He probably won't remember a word I've said when he wakes up again.

I walk to the window. Shadows waver on ice and snow and despite the early hour, despite the cold, people walk the streets. A man dressed in a long wool coat and wide brim hat looks upward, catches my eyes and I swear his eyes turn red. A demon beneath my window or just a trick of the light? I draw the blinds. A howling rises from below. Just my imagination making the wind into something it isn't, I tell myself. But I still feel the fear coursing through me and wonder if I'll always feel so scared.

I go back to my chair, spread my coat over my knees and close my eyes. I think about Heaven and Hell, unsure of where things are going, and if they'll spiral out of control.

I welcome sleep, and promise myself that tomorrow I'll face the world. I'll deal with it no matter what.

13

I must have fallen into a deep sleep, because when I awakened the sun was out. Snow falls lightly again, and the radio weatherman says two storms have already passed over New York. Another is on its way, which explains why snowfall has been so erratic over the past couple of days. Rico stands in the middle of my living room, hair soaking wet, towel wrapped around his waist. He drinks coffee with a faraway look in his eyes, reminds me of a figure in a painting I once saw at the Met. It was at an exhibit of American art from the industrial revolution. Several paintings depicted black people tilling fields and working on the railroad. The men all had sullen dark eyes and large hands. The hardship of their daily lives was etched across their faces, but their strength and dignity was just as evident, in the way their backs arched, in the way they stood proud, yet struggling, always struggling. Poor sweet Rico has that same look, those same kinds of scars oppression and degradation inflict on a person. I wonder if he thinks about it all, or if his literal day-to-day survival requires his total focus.

"Morning," he says when he sees me staring at him. "Man, that shower felt good. Street life makes it hard to stay well-groomed, ya know?"

I notice a gold chain around his neck. Three turquoise stones encased in gold hang from it. "Did you get that from my sister? It looks like one she had."

He touches the stones. "Yeah, called me over one night, said she was cleaning things out."

"Looks good on you. Did you save me some coffee?"

"I'll get you a cup." He drops the towel and reaches for the jeans he'd tossed on the floor. Rico is good looking, slender and his skin is smooth and toned. It doesn't embarrass me seeing him naked. He's gay and I have an affinity for straight perpetual losers who treat me like shit. I watch him strut into the kitchen. He's humming. The man has no home, no family, he's penniless and a murder suspect to boot, but he hums.

"Sugar?" he yells. "Milk?"

"Lots of both."

"You going to work?" He starts to hum again.

"Shit, no." I reach for the phone and dial my supervisor's number so I can call in sick. It's seven-thirty and she won't be in until eight, so if I leave a message I won't have to answer questions, won't have to hear her sigh impatiently at the thought of not having a full staff. Her life is consumed by her cubicle and the documents spread across her desk, by the actions of her subordinates. All day long she bows her head over her PC as though she's praying to God. She gives this God her soul. Her heart beats for Him and she allows Him to cloud her mind, to dull her passions. What a leech the bastard is.

The phone rings three times. The machine kicks in. "You have reached the office of Rita Somsby. I'm not in the office right now. Please leave a message after the beep."

The beep is metallic, harsh. I make my best effort to sound sick. "Rita, it's Gina. I was up all night, sick to my stomach, must be the flu that's going round. I won't be in. Bye."

"You sounded like a cat in heat." Rico is standing in front of me. He's wearing my red hat and a pair of red angora mittens. "Found these on the kitchen table. I love them." He looks silly and he tries not to laugh as he bends slightly to serve me a steaming cup of coffee. "Meow," he whines in a high-pitched voice. "Cat in heat, that's all I could think of when you were on the phone."

"I was trying to sound sick." I take a sip of coffee. It's good.

"You sounded sick, believe me." He's got the hat on backwards and the gloves are too tight for his large hands. He's twirling around the room like a drunken drag queen. I begin to laugh and can't stop. Tony didn't have a sense of humor. I couldn't kid around with him and realize now how much I missed laughing.

He stops, hands on hips. "I saw Detective Harris cruising back and forth down the street before you woke up." Rico sits across from me, plucks off the hat then removes the mittens slowly as though he's doing a striptease act. "That man thinks I'm a natural born killer. He doesn't know I'm Queen Rico."

I wonder if he dresses in drag and goes downtown to hang with the girls by the underpass, dangling fingers decorated with rhinestone rings and waving wrists with bangle bracelets.

"I can't shake the dude, ya know." Rico looks to the window.

"He's just looking out for me. That's all."

"Not sure that's all it is, the way he checks you out."

"How's he check me out?"

"Like he's hot for you."

"You're so full of it." I cradle the coffee cup in my hands. The warmth feels good. "I keep thinking of our conversation before, about the black chick and photographing ghosts and stuff."

"I thought that was a dream. I think we both might have had the same dream at the same time." Rico's face is serious now. "Ever try photographing your boyfriend Tony?"

"I tried, but the shots either came out too dark, too blurry, too something. He's the only significant person in my life that—"

"I dreamed last night that Harris hauled my ass to Rikers," Rico interrupts.

"Just another dream."

"Maybe, but my dreams come true sometimes." He leans back. His eyes are bloodshot, dark circles surround them. The mood has shifted. The snow is falling heavily again.

"Well, we're two of a kind then." I'm glad Rico is here.

Last night would have been horrible without him.

"The church. Ever snoop around inside there?" He's looking at Allie's painting, maybe trying to figure out its message.

I shake my head. "I've done a lot of photography there. That's all. Every time I've been close to checking it out, Daniel—I mean Detective Harris—shows up."

"Daniel, huh?" He chuckles softly. "Let's grab a train up to Harlem, girl. Maybe what's ailing both of us is in there."

"I'm too tired."

"Being tired is bullshit." He pulls his sweater over his head, grabs his coat and quickly slips it on. He picks my coat off the floor. "Come on, put this on."

He throws my coat over my shoulders, slaps my hat on my head, hands me my purse and leads me to the door. I wrap a scarf around my neck, button my coat and follow Rico down the stars. "What put a fire up your ass?" I can't keep up with him. He has long legs and he takes two stairs at a time.

He turns then stops, allowing me to catch up. "Just a gut feeling I'm having, girl. Humor me."

I don't say another word as we go out the door and onto icy pavement. We walk a block then duck down subway stairs. Trains rumble, the homeless walk like zombies with outstretched hands and dark things slither on the tracks. It's so cold, but—

"I dreamed it," Rico says, breaking my concentration. "Don't ask too many questions."

"What?" An incoming train is rolling to a stop. "I didn't say anything."

Am I dreaming now?

Rico grabs my hand. "Come on."

The subway stops in front of us, its doors open and people exit, walking as though they're half alive—or half dead—carrying brief cases, wearing black coats and hats, staring straight ahead with vacant eyes.

We climb onboard and take a seat. The lights go out as we begin to move, and I find myself wondering why Rico is suddenly so motivated, what this day will bring, and if we'll survive it.

14

The subway lights flash on then off and we're submerged in darkness again. Footsteps shuffle across the train, and what sounds like a large package or bag drops to the floor nearby. I hear a familiar female voice across from us. The voice is soft and shaky. "This is scary, we should have taken a bus, or a cab."

No one answers the woman.

As the subway continues, shaking and rumbling beneath the ground, I imagine the people above us, see them walking in the brilliance of a snowy day, oblivious to what's happening below them. Maybe Hell is closer than we all realize. Maybe it's nothing more than an endless subway ride in murky blackness, the passengers trapped within and longing to one day return to a world that revolves around a life-giving sun. Maybe Hell is a planet no one speaks of, a spinning ball of sin and evil existing alongside us just behind the veil of death and inhabited by the vilest creatures in existence. Maybe those creatures are able to move between their world and ours. Or maybe, just maybe, it all belongs to them and there's not a damn thing we can do about it.

The lights suddenly come on, revealing two passengers sitting across from us. My sister's friend, Lisa, and another woman with a ski mask pulled over her face. Lisa's eyes dart back and forth, and she's paler than I remember. It looks as though she's made a pointless attempt to straighten her unruly hair, as several straight and uneven pieces hang around her haggard face. Her bangs are greasy ringlets and the rest of her locks are a thick maze of frizz and clumpy waves. She holds her companion's hand the way a child holds a parent's. I look closer and notice Lisa wears a black lace jacket that used to be Allie's. It's tight around her chest and waist, and her short leather skirt—once Lisa's as well—is skintight, emphasizing her disproportionate legs even more. She starts to cry, and as the tears streak her face, her thick makeup begins to smudge and run. She doesn't seem to notice me even though I'm right in front of her. "I don't like taking the subway," Lisa says to her companion. "I told you."

Her companion turns to her. "Shut the fuck up, you whiney bitch," she says with a hiss. "You weren't complaining back in my bed."

I wonder why Lisa hasn't noticed me. Is she so wrapped up in suffering, in self-absorption that she can't focus on her surroundings? Her companion does notice me, and smiles. Though the ski mask covers her face, the hole where her mouth is reveals a smile and set of teeth that look oddly familiar to me.

A dozen or more people have moved into the car, apparently having crossed over from another compartment during the blackout.

Lisa looks around the subway, still not seeing me or Rico but studying the others with intensity now. Like a sacrificial lamb waiting to be slaughtered by witches on a blood moon night, she watches the others with nervous uncertainty.

I follow her gaze and notice the other passengers more closely myself. They do seem unnatural upon closer inspection. It's subtle but unmistakable. Abnormal and humped over, with elongated fingers clutching turnstiles and sitting cross-legged on benches, they all seem to be laughing at Lisa, shaking their heads. This is New York. People don't give a shit about your sexuality or what you're talking about on the subway, and yet...

I turn to Rico. "Something's wrong. This train, it—"

"We've stepped over some fucked up boundary line or something." He clutches my arm and I can feel the fear in him. "We're getting off at the next stop. We'll get a cab. You got money?"

"Yeah." I bite my lip in the hopes it might stop my trembling. "Why doesn't Lisa know me?"

"She doesn't know me either. I've met her a hundred times." Rico looks toward the platform as the train slows. "But things are different here."

The subway comes to a screeching halt. "We're at Columbus Circle," I whisper to him. "There are lots of stops between Canal and here. We should've stopped earlier."

The movement of passengers distracts me, and I turn to see them crowding around Lisa and her companion. The woman in the ski mask begins rubbing Lisa's legs, slowly pushing Lisa's skirt up over her hips to expose a thick patch of pubic hair covering bulbous pink lips. She reaches over and roughly spreads Lisa's legs.

"Not here," Lisa whimpers.

Her companion slips off the ski mask. Her spiked hair glistens with sweat. Blood drips from a ring in her nose. Though Lisa struggles a bit at first, the bizarre men and women greedily take turns pushing fingers inside her, fondling her, and she eventually begins to move with their thrusts. She moans then screams, and I can't figure out if Lisa's slack mouth and upturned eyes imply pleasure, pain or both.

The train halts and Rico and I flee for the open door. As the train begins to move again blood sprays the windows, spattering them violently.

"Don't look," Rico says, pulling me along with him before I have time to scream. "Come on!"

We run across the platform, passing people who seemingly walk as though they're barely alive, past others leaning against benches, skeletal faces still and dead. We climb the stairs and head into light. We breathe deeply as a blast of snow greets us.

Rico turns to me as we slow to a fast-walk. "Gina, you know, don't you?"

"Know what?" I ask, still looking behind us every few seconds to make sure none of those things are following us. "Lisa, you know about Lisa, right?"

"What about her, I—"

"They found her dead outside a bar on Lex a few months back. Somebody cut her up real bad down there. You know, down *there*." He points to his crotch. "That wasn't Lisa back on that train, just somebody who looked like her. And those people weren't people at all."

"It was like Hell," I tell him.

"Lisa's Hell," Rico corrects me as he blesses himself, making the sign of the cross. "Your sister, she was like us, she saw things and shit, but she was evil and that evil gave those fucked up things life.

She fucked around with shit, with bad people, bad magic."

"What the fuck are you talking about?" I want to scream, I want to stop and rest, I want to clear my head and think, but I just keep moving along the street with him. "My sister was weird, eccentric—shit—maybe even crazy at times, but she wasn't evil."

"Girl, you know she was. You know it."

And I do. He's right, I just don't want to admit it, don't want to think of my sister in those terms. I feel drained and lightheaded, like I need to sit down and sleep until this all goes away. "You think she's responsible for what went down back there?" I ask. "You think she's behind everything that's been happening?"

Rico nods.

"But how?"

"I don't know if it was all her," he says. "We got to go to the church."

He steps off the curb and hails a cab. Before I can question him or object, he hustles me inside, joins me in the backseat and gives the driver directions to the old church in Harlem.

The cab lurches forward, we move through the traffic. "Didn't tell you this before," Rico explains, staring straight ahead and speaking slowly. "But your sister had lots of lovers, OK? I've been thinking about how she acted the last time I saw her, some shit she said. She had a lover, some guy from Harlem. He was special, not some cheap thrill or a one-night stand. I don't know his real name, never met him, but she told me about him, called him by some weird nickname. I can't fucking remember what though. She said he was some sort of witch doctor, into voodoo or some shit like that. She said it was cool, that she was learning a whole new religion." He turns, looks me in the eye. "But maybe it was more than that."

"Probably a bunch of bullshit, that's all. She made stuff up all the time. The guy was probably a minister or something boring, Allie always exaggerated, you know that." I think of the wild tales Allie invented when we were kids. She loved horror movies and books. I assure myself she must've been jiving Rico.

"No, *listen* to me." Rico shakes his head in frustration. "I knew some old ladies from Spanish Harlem. They did a lot of magic with roots and stones, cured stiff joints and made women fertile—that kind of shit—but they said there's a dark side to magic, always a dark side. Some people get obsessed, self-absorbed. Things can work out fine if you do it right. You can get you all kinds of stuff—money, nice cars, good sex, power—you name it. But if you don't do it right then literally—and I mean *literally*—all fucking Hell can break loose." Rico looks scared again. "Allie said her man was sacrificing chickens during his ceremonies. Who knows, maybe he started in on people next. Maybe that's what the mess was they found in the church."

"You think things got that fucked up?" I keep picturing Lisa back on that train, living in a hell created just for her. "That Allie got caught up in the shit this guy was doing and—"

"Last time I saw your sister she was scared, said this warlock—or whatever the fuck he was—went over the edge. Said he was crazy."

"Why the hell didn't you tell me any of this before?"

Rico shrugs uncomfortably and scratches at himself nervously, reminding me of his addictions, his afflictions. "I forget things sometimes, I—things get cloudy on me. You know how it is. Maybe I brushed it off, I don't know. Maybe I didn't want to remember, didn't think I needed to until now. Whatever, I'm telling you now, OK?" Rico leans back and sighs. "And it fits together like pieces of a puzzle."

"So, Allie got mixed up with a psycho, some guy she should've stayed clear of and—and some people got killed. It doesn't mean—"

"If it's that simple then what's all this shit we keep seeing?"

I stare into his eyes, but have no answer for him.

Rico wipes his nose with the sleeve of his coat. I fish a Kleenex out of my purse and hand it to him. He takes it and blows his nose loudly.

The cab slows down, pulls over to the curb. The old church leers down at us.

I pay the driver and we step out of the cab. Standing on the sidewalk like two lost children trying to figure out our next move, we watch the church as the cab pulls away, leaving us alone in a desolate part of the city.

For a moment, the beautiful woman from my dreams waves at us from the church doorway, but then she's gone and only a splintered, weather-beaten door remains.

"I'm losing my fucking mind," I mumble.

"No," Rico tells me softly. "I saw her too."

I nearly cry. We can't both be insane. "Really?"

"I told you I see her just like you," he says. "She's trying to tell us something. I think she might have gotten caught up in all this somehow."

"Just like us," I say.

Rico nods and offers his hand. I take it, and together, we slowly climb the church steps.

15

Rico pushes open the church door, moves ahead of me then motions with his hand for me to stand back as he looks around. He turns to look at me and smiles weakly. "Seems ok," he says. "Out here anyway."

I follow him into a crowded entranceway and smell dampness, wax and incense. There are plaster saints lining the walls: Saint Joan of Arc in her armor, Mary holding an infant wearing a golden crown, Saint Christopher carrying a beautiful child on his back, and others I recognize from religious study. But there are also African warrior Gods here I don't recognize. They tower above us and seem to mock us with cold painted eyes. "Isn't this an old Baptist church? Catholic Saints mixed with African Gods seem inappropriate."

Rico's eyes are filled with amusement now. "You read any of those books back at your apartment?"

"I'll get around to it."

"Well, when you do you'll learn that lots of people that came from the islands—from Africa too—combined different beliefs, blended the old beliefs with Christianity." He looks around. "Seems like they just collected shit from everywhere, must have been one of the churches that honored Christ on Sundays and did Voodoo or Santeria at other times." He focuses on a strange black figure wearing a triple crown. It rests against a wooden carving of a Goddess with three heads. "I've been here before, but never noticed," he says as he turns next to the massive statue of Joan of Arc.

I'm afraid to look at any of them, afraid that when I turn away I'll see statues moving out of the corner of my eye. At any moment, they'll leap from their pedestals and attack us. It reminds me of a nightmare I had as a child about statues coming alive and chasing me into a dark forest. Those memories combined with my nervousness over being in the church in the first place leave me spooked, and I decide to keep a safe distance between the statues and myself just to play it safe.

Rico is bolder than I. He touches the foot of Saint Joan and studies her armor. "Tough chick, but she's creepy, gotta admit that. Lots of this religious shit is." He laughs and points to the sword at her side. "She might get me with that thing. Reminds me of something I heard when I was a kid—just a story about witches—was up in Canada somewhere. They all used to get together on Halloween and shit. They made little saints out of clay and then put the heebie-jeebies on them, did all these curses, you know. Then they turned around and sold them at county fairs, at church bazaars. Mothers used to buy them for kid's rooms and put them on bureaus and tables by their beds. At night, the things started haunting them with bad dreams, scaring the shit out of them when they woke up."

"Stop it."

"Hey, it's just a story."

"Not now, OK?"

He nods, looks into Saint Joan's eyes and turns away. I swear her lips move. I swear I hear her mumbling something incoherent.

We move deeper inside the church. Once again Rico takes the lead, checking things out before motioning me to his side. "Check this out," he says. A woman's black cape is draped on a folding chair in a corner, and a man's top hat rests on it. Hymnals lie on dusty sills. It all looks as if it's been here for decades, exactly as people left them. But next to the items several tapered candles burn on a wrought iron holder. "Ain't seen that before. Somebody's been here," Rico says. He points to several silver coins scattered on the floor.

"Maybe someone was lost or caught in the storm," I suggest, "looking for shelter and for strength from prayer?"

Snow falls across a broken skylight above us, the flakes shimmering as they catch candlelight and blend with smoke and dust. A huge wooden cross is propped against the altar, and crime scene tape lies in ribbons throughout the church. There are chalk markings on walls and on the floor, and deep vermillion stains streak wooden planks and spatter walls. A figure of Christ seems to look right through me with soulful eyes. Blood trickles from His nail wounds and a crown of thorns pierces His forehead and skull. Plaster angels flank the altar; eyes turned upward, hands clasped in perpetual prayer.

Rico and I move down the center aisle. Dead flowers are strewn in pews, stained glass windows are cracked and faded, and clay bowls and used candles lay in a pile on a smaller altar by the church's rear exit. There are fresh flowers inside a crystal vase and herbs before a strange wooden carving. "African God," Rico says. He picks up the object and turns it over in his hands. "I think it's evil, bad news."

Something familiar catches my eye, a tin of coffee next to the carving. Island Blend From Jamaica. It's decorated with yellow parrots and colored chameleons. My sister gave me several cans months ago. I drink it all the time. She told me a friend brought back suitcases of it after a trip to Jamaica. I've never seen it anywhere else. "Look familiar?" I ask Rico.

He nods. "Allie's blend. I had some at my place too. Police took it, I guess. Good stuff though." He looks around. "We're not alone. This place is haunted, don't you feel it?"

Floorboards creak and the church seems to get darker as if in answer. Shadows that weren't at the altar moments ago are moving in the candlelight now. As Rico and I stand there mesmerized, trying to understand what's happening all around us, the shadowy images become more concrete and begin to take shape. A couple appears before my eyes. I recognize the beautiful woman as the same person from my dreams. Wearing the black cape I'd seen draped over the folding chair, she kneels at the altar, a songbook clutched in her hands as a ghostly voice erupts, bringing forth music both somber and eerie. A man wearing a black top hat stands beside her. He touches her shoulder, and she turns and looks our way. Her lips move slowly, her words drifting into this world like the falling snow. "Nothing is as it seems. Leave this street in Harlem before the Mojo Man takes your soul like he took mine." The vision dissipates and it is replaced by swirling snow.

"Did you see her?" I ask. "Who's Mojo Man? Did you hear her?"

I can't be sure he has, but there is a level of fear in Rico's eyes that wasn't there before. His hand shakes when he touches mine. "Mojo Man, I think that's what your sister called that guy, can't remember for sure—"

I hear movement in the entranceway. It sounds as though someone has jumped onto the cement floor. Snow falling from the broken skylight intensifies and one of the stone angels shifts on her pedestal, stretches long fingers and begins to stroke her harp. Blood drops fall from the strings and she weeps like a lost child. "Rico, do you..."

He stares at the wooden crucifix, as if in a trance now, and I can only wonder what he sees. I hear a strange sound in the distance, an odd wailing noise that gets louder and louder until it sounds as if it's right on top of us. Rico jumps and blinks his eyes. "Sirens," he says dully. "Fucking sirens."

Suddenly people are talking, there are voices everywhere and someone seems to be giving orders. Fists bang on wood and the door springs open. We both turn quickly to see Daniel standing in the doorway. Snow swirls behind him as several of New York's finest scatter about the church. Two officers remain at Daniel's side. Red and blue lights reflect from the street behind them. "Rico, step away from the girl." Daniel's face is stoic as he draws his weapon, assumes a shooting stance and moves slowly down the aisle. His semi-automatic is aimed directly at Rico's head. "Make me tell you again and I'll blow your fucking head off."

Rico confusedly steps aside and raises his hands. "Whoa, man, take it easy. I ain't done nothing." Daniel's stride quickens, and when he reaches Rico he turns him and pushes him against the wall.

"What the fuck?" Rico snaps. "This ain't breaking and entering, it's a church. Sanctuary and all that shit, man, what's wrong with you?"

"It's a crime scene, and the only kind of sanctuary you'll be getting is at Rikers. Turn around and put your hands behind your back." Rico obeys and Daniel handcuffs him. "Rico Patterson, you're under arrest. You have the right to remain—"

"Fuck, man, I couldn't kill a canary. You got no evidence against me."

Daniel reaches inside Rico's jacket then inside his shirt and pulls out the turquoise necklace. "This belonged to a woman named Lucia Martineau. We found her dead in this church."

"No, it belonged to Allie. She gave it to me. You're wrong."

"It was handmade for Lucia. Her father gave it to her when she graduated from high school. He said she never took it off. Wanted to know if we'd found it when he viewed the body at the morgue. There's only one like it. We found more evidence at your office, other trophies. We busted open walls, tore up the floors. You're fucked."

"Man, I've been set up." Rico turns to me. "Gina, you gotta tell him Allie was fucking evil. She did this to me, gave me all kinds of shit, set me up. Gotta be. Gina, no matter what, don't lose touch with me, come see me in that hellhole they're bringing me to. You gotta help me."

"I will," I say as Daniel pushes Rico again. "Stop it, you don't have to be so rough with him, he's not resisting."

"We've been watching you," Daniel says to Rico, as if he didn't hear me. "Followed you here, just like we do every day. Usually we'd let you light your candles and do your thing but we couldn't take any chances today, not with the girl, not with the new evidence." He spins Rico away from the wall and into the hands of two waiting officers. "Get this scum out of here."

"Man, I haven't been here, haven't lit any candles. I was with Gina, sleeping at her place last night. You fucking know that."

"You were here the other night, the night before, and the night before that. Kids from the projects wandered in earlier then ran out of here like banshees according to the plainclothes guys watching this place. They must've rekindled the candles before they ran."

"Bull-fucking-shit!" Rico's eyes fill with tears. "I'm innocent!"

"You're a killer and a liar." Daniel nods to one of the officers. "Franco, get him out of my face."

The two policemen escort Rico from the church none too gently as he continues to call my name and protest his innocence.

Daniel takes my arm and guides me outside. I'm so pissed off I can't even look at him. We watch as they push Rico into a squad car. "Gina!" he yells, "Don't forget about me, don't lose touch! Don't leave me in there! Don't leave me!"

And then he's in the car, the doors slam shut and the cruiser drives away.

"I'm sick to my stomach," I tell Daniel. "Rico's no killer. This is all a mistake."

"He's doomed," Daniel says. "He's getting the needle." He looks back at the church. "Place gives me the creeps. Are you OK?"

"He's not a killer. You treated him with no respect. He didn't deserve that."

Daniel turns to me. There's anger in his face, but his voice softens when he speaks to me. "All the evidence points to him, Gina."

"I don't give a shit what points to him, Rico's innocent."

"That's for a jury to decide, my job's just to get him off the street. Don't sweat it. You're safe now."

"I was always safe with him. He wouldn't hurt me, he wouldn't hurt anyone. Look, I know Rico. I think maybe my sister did set him up. She may have even set me and a lot of other people up too. That necklace, I saw it at my sister's place. Rico was telling the truth, she gave it to him."

"There's lots of jewelry that looks similar to it. You can buy it on Broadway for two bucks. This chick's got racks of it, all different color stones. The one Rico was wearing had a real gold chain, real turquoise. Couldn't have been the same one your sister had."

"I saw it, and I'll swear to that," I insist, but I begin to doubt myself. Did Allie's necklace have a gold chain? Were the stones real?

Daniel looks straight ahead, ignoring me. "Are you hungry? My shift's up, can I buy you lunch? Bet you haven't even had breakfast yet today. You look like you haven't eaten or slept in days."

"I'm not going anywhere with you. Just get me a cab, or take me to a bus stop. And don't fucking drive by my apartment again. I don't need your protection."

"Gina, cool off. At least let me take you home."

He tries to take my arm but I yank it away. "Fine." The storm has gotten worse. I'll take his ride back downtown, but that's it. "Take me home then."

He opens the car door and I get in. Neither of us speaks as he pulls away from the church.

When we reach 125th Street he says, "That whole street back there, there's lots of stories about it. It's a perfect place for murder, perfect place to feed a lunatic's sick longings."

"Rico's no lunatic, he's good people." After a moment I ask, "What kind of stories?"

"Turn of the century a family from Jamaica came to New York. They had money and they bought up all the houses on that street. Rumor has it a man named Mojo DeCanne made his money back on the islands illegally—some say dope, others say bootlegging—who the hell knows what's true and what isn't? He practiced Voodoo. The whole family did." A traffic light turns red and we come to a stop. "From everything I've always read about it, Voodoo is a healing religion that's been unfairly stigmatized by Hollywood and old novels. Most people think it's evil, but far as I know it's not any better or worse than any other religion. Still, some people twist it and use its power for all the wrong things. Supposedly some groups get involved in human sacrifice. DeCanne was guilty of that. He'd hold ceremonies in that church, killing for the blood. He said it gave him power. Guy killed hundreds of people, mostly poor immigrants lured to their deaths with promises of food and money. It went on for years."

"How'd he get away with murdering people like that?"

"Church got raided for something or other one night, gambling, prostitution, DeCanne ran all his business from that church. Sick, really sick. Anyway, the cops got more than they bargained for during that raid. They found bones and decomposing bodies in the basement. They were stacked one on top of the other. It was a slaughterhouse. DeCanne got sent upstate, died in the electric chair, but he told people all the blood, all the killings, gave him power to overcome death as we know it and how it would allow him to come back, would allow him to bring other dead, demons and maybe the Devil himself back with him. That, my girl, is fucking perversion."

"And you think Rico did shit like that? He wouldn't step on a bug. Are you out of your mind?"

Daniel gives me an annoyed sideways glance. "I think he got wrapped up in the stories, in the legends that DeCanne could raise the dead, could have power over others. Evidence says Rico killed a lot of people, Gina."

"You're wrong. He's a sweet guy down on his luck, that's all. He's an easy mark for somebody like you."

"Somebody like me, huh?" He seems amused by this. The light turns red and Daniel lifts his hands off the steering wheel then slams them back down so violently it startles me. He pulls into traffic, almost hitting a yellow cab before he fishtails down Fifth. "Look, you think you're the only one who ever lost a sister? I lost my kid sister to a maniac like Rico. Whole family thought he was a nice guy, always coming to the house to pick up my sister, always getting her home by the time my father wanted, even told us he moved here from Philly, was going to Parsons to be a designer. My mother loved the sonofabitch, and she of all people normally knows when something isn't right, she can pick out a loser a mile away. One night this guy didn't take my sister home, and two days later they found her dead in an empty house in Queens. This fucking creep lived there, was sleeping in that house and eating his meals there with my sister's body propped up on his living room couch. Three other bodies were found buried in the back yard. Yeah, he was a real fucking sweet guy down on his luck too."

"I'm sorry," I tell him. "I truly am, Daniel, but I'm telling you as someone who knows him, Rico isn't capable of such things."

"Look, get it through your head that he's a con, a master at pulling the wool over people's eyes, OK? I deal with scum like him all the time, I know how they work. They get people to trust them and then they move in and steal and exploit and sometimes even murder if it suits their purposes. And they're almost always aligned with an innocent like you. They'll mutilate and torture your sister, your kids and your mother, because they're brains are wired by the fucking Devil himself."

"Not Rico. I've known him a long time. I've—"

"Wake up. Stop being such a pushover."

"I'm not a pushover. You don't know me."

"I know a million girls like you. White, pretty, from nice middle-class families. You were raised with blinders on. You don't see the real world like I do every single day."

"Oh, give me a break."

"Just wake up or you'll never survive in this city."

"What the hell makes you think I need you to tell me how to survive this city? I've survived it just fine so far. And has it ever occurred to you that you could be wrong about Rico? We all make mistakes."

"Get a grip."

"Enough. I'm sorry about your sister, ok? I know you must deal with horrible shit every day, and I'm sorry you have to go through that, but—"

"But, nothing. I did the right thing tonight. You'll see that soon enough."

"I'm tired of talking about it. Fuck you, ok?" It feels good, swearing at him like that. I wait for a reaction, for a sign that I've hurt him, for more angry words in exchange, but he doesn't answer. He just keeps driving.

We move through Harlem, in and out of streets where old brownstones still stand majestically showcasing the fine craftsmanship of New York's early days. We turn onto Fifth Avenue. It looks beautiful, gleaming with snow, lights blinking and people walking shoulder to shoulder. I begin to feel as if we've finally left that awful darkness behind.

I watch a bleak landscape through the window as we move through mid-town, past the New York Public Library and on past Macy's on 34th, down Broadway past all my favorite shops in Soho. The snow is blinding now and no one's on the streets down here.

Daniel eases his car in front of my apartment. If I weren't so pissed I'd invite him up, be more concerned about his drive back home. But not this time. I can't give him that satisfaction, not while Rico's hurting, being interrogated by police, maybe even being brutalized for all I know. Poor Rico.

"You piss me off, kid," he says with a sigh. "For a lot of reasons, I shouldn't care what happens, shouldn't let this shit eat away at me, but I'll be around, OK? Somebody's got to look out for you," he says softly. His eyes are intense, anger still burns within them.

I don't say a word as I slide out of his car then slam the door. I watch him drive away, taillights piercing through white, car fishtailing down the avenue. I picture him driving around in the storm all night, lost in a city he knows too well, feeling guilt for what he did to an innocent man.

A longing tugs at my heart and I begin to cry as I climb my front stairs. I wish I could hug Rico, comfort him and keep him warm. I hope the bad things don't seek him out in the darkness of the storm while he sleeps later tonight, hissing and taunting him in dreams, in the dark.

Alone in the storm, I lie down on my couch and decompress. Maybe I'll go to work tomorrow; maybe I'll never go back again. Either way, if I'm lucky I'll nod off and sleep undisturbed all day and deep into the night.

But then again, I've never been all that lucky.

16

Gina, wake up.

"Why are you sleeping in the middle of the day?"

"Allie?" I sit up. It's freezing in here. It's dark, so dark, but I can see my sister sitting across from me. "You're alive."

Allie takes her cue, leaning forward to speak. Smoky tendrils escape her lips and cloudy halos surround her hands each time she moves. "I'm not sure."

"How did you get here?"

Rather than answer me she says, "Hey, still got that coffee I gave you?"

"Yeah, lots of it."

"Too much is no good. Maybe you should switch to tea." She smiles.

I notice she's wearing a pair of ripped jeans. Her jacket is torn at the sleeve and there's a smear of something on her face that looks like dried blood. "Are you OK?"

"Better than ever. I've been wandering around the city, just taking in shit, you know? There's so many pathetic chicks here, I never realized it before. You know, a guy says 'hi' to them or holds a door open and they think the guy's hot for them. They think they're fucking shit 'cause they got a little bit of attention. Truth is they're fucking ordinary, with nothing lives so any attention they get, anytime somebody notices them, they get all giggly, act like they're going to cream their fucking pants." Allie shakes her head. Her beautiful hair sways, framing her pale face. A lock falls over her right eye. She doesn't push it away. She merely sighs and looks toward the window. "Tough out there when you're ordinary."

I rub my eyes. There's a message here, a clue to what's happening.

"Where are you, what—where have you been? What did they do to you?"

"My body? Nobody knows, and I've lost touch." She taps her fingers on the chair's armrest as if bored. When she moves her hand away small droplets of blood remain. Another slow trickle of blood leaks from her lips.

"They arrested Rico," I tell her. "Did you know that?"

"He's changed, did *you* know *that*?" Her eyelids flutter and she rests her head against the back of the chair. "I can't stay here too much longer. They'll come looking and they can't find me, not yet."

I want to hug her, but I fear she'll take me back to wherever she came from. I just want to keep her talking. "Rico's changed?"

She stands, swaying a bit. "I see Tony in the city. Ever wonder why the photos you took of him are never clear? I see that woman, the pretty one you dream about." Allie steps to the side then backs away, toward the door. Her feet aren't touching the floor. "We're all in limbo."

Her body suddenly slams against the door, as if yanked back violently by invisible strings. On impact, she shatters to pieces like a china doll. Shards fly off in different directions, pieces of my sister destroyed, lost, doomed.

I scream her name as a heavy thudding sound brings me back, rips me from the darkness.

My eyes focus and I realize I'm still lying on the couch. It feels like early evening but I can't be sure. Someone's pounding on the door. I sit up, look to the chair where Allie was sitting just seconds before.

"Gina? Are you all right?" Daniel's voice. From his tone, it sounds like he's been knocking for some time. He knocks again, three times, rattling the door.

"What do you want?" I yell out.

"Weather's bad. Way bad. The city's closed down. Brooklyn Bridge is closed. I can't get home."

"So, go back to the station," I tell him. I hate this gnawing attraction I feel for him. I should hate him. I do hate him. "Sleep at your desk or something."

"Come on, Gina, open the door, I want to talk to you."

"Yeah? Well, I want my sister back," I mutter. "I want Rico to be free." I move to the door, open it slowly. Daniel's soaked from head to toe. He's shivering. "What?"

He smiles at me. "Was hoping I could get some more of that tea."

I stare at him.

"Gina, I wish you could understand—"

"Don't you know any other pathetic and ordinary women who need attention?"

"You're far from ordinary," he says softly. He waits for me to allow him inside. Tony would have just pushed his way in.

I open the door wider, roll my eyes and with a sigh, motion him in. "Come on."

He stands on the threshold, his jacket rolled up under his arm and his boots dripping. Even now he waits for me to again invite him deeper inside the apartment.

I think about Rico, wonder where he is now. He's probably locked up in the precinct jail. The weather's too bad for a trip to Rikers.

Daniel stands before the books I haven't read yet, another odd and unexplainable attraction. "Nice book collection," he says. "Have you read them all?"

"I haven't read any of them."

He chuckles. "Well, I know a lot about these things. I studied a lot of this stuff. Shit that goes on in the city, you know. People with strange beliefs coming from even stranger places that sometimes don't even realize they're doing harm or breaking the law. It's good to have a background."

I smile. Maybe the two strange attractions in my life— books and men—are one in the same. Daniel could be a perfect lover and friend if he hadn't jumped to conclusions about Rico, if he'd bothered to find out the truth. I watch him as his fingers touch the book bindings and his eyes glide from title to title.

Perhaps he has something to reveal. Just like my dreams.

17

It looks as though it's snowing harder. New York is a world of white, distant and separated on this night from the rest of the country, far from all of humanity. The TV weatherman says the snow won't stop until tomorrow, that there's another front coming down from Canada and if the temperature doesn't rise it'll snow for the next few days.

"This is crazy." Daniel sighs then looks to the window. "My grandfather used to tell me about storms like this, how they crippled the city back in the old days. He used to work in old warehouses out in Brooklyn, said it was always freezing in winter, said during storms they'd work through the night, sometimes with no light, no nothing.

"Things were tough. I figured with technology it couldn't happen these days. Guess there's no escaping extreme weather no matter how smart or modern the world has become." He rubs his hands together. "How about that tea?"

I'm happy he's here, and I want to know more about his family, his past. I'll gladly oblige his simple needs for now. "I'll boil some water. I've got a stockpile of food in the cupboards. I'm a packrat when it comes to canned goods, cereals and stuff like that. We won't starve."

He smiles. "That's a good thing. My grandmother had a basement full of canned goods, more boxes of paper towels and toilet paper than she'd use in her lifetime. My mother said it's because she lived through the depression, still had that mindset." His voice is distant. He plucks a book from the case, turns several pages then puts it back. He chooses another book and turns to the table of contents.

"Interesting." He looks to the window, shakes his head.

I wonder if he's sorry he came here. "Want something to eat now?" I ask.

He rubs his hand over the book's cover. "Maybe later, thanks."

"Sorry. I often feel the need to feed handsome men and cute furry animals."

He smiles. "Tea and the book are fine for now."

I leave Daniel sitting on the living room couch absorbed in a book on Caribbean magic, wearing reading glasses he told me he'd bought in a dollar store on West Broadway.

I'll go downstairs later and check with Frankie, see if they've got food. It's quiet down there. His girlfriend isn't singing and she's not talking loud like she normally does.

I pour clean water in the kettle. The water pressure is weaker than normal. I set the kettle on the stove and light the burner. As I shut the water off the pipes make odd groaning noises. I wonder if Frankie's working on them down in the basement or something.

"That super of yours responsible for those pipes?"

Daniel is standing in the doorway, his glasses resting at the tip of his nose. He's unbuttoned his shirt and his hair, still damp from the snow, is tousled. It looks soft.

"Yeah, I was going to take a walk down there, see what's going on. His girlfriend stirs up concoctions in her big old pot. I doubt it's chicken soup or anything nourishing."

Daniel moves farther into the kitchen, tucks his hands in his pockets and listens for a moment as a tinny sound emerges from below. "I'll go with you. Maybe he needs help or something, never know. Pipes freeze in weather like this. Sounds like hell. I'm not sure what happens before they freeze, but it's best to check with him."

"Sit, drink your tea. No one's going anywhere, so have something warm before we go down."

"Yes ma'am." He pulls out a chair and smiles. "You still mad at me?"

"Look, Rico is a special guy. I don't want to argue with you, not now, not while we have to spend God knows how long together like this, but I think the arrest is a big mistake. Somebody framed him. Somebody screwed up."

"You think I screwed up?" He doesn't look at me, just stares at his hands.

"I've been thinking a lot. I think my sister set things up. I think she fucked with people and their lives. I had a dream about her right before you got here. It was so real, like she wasn't dead. Maybe she had these magical powers and she put stuff in my head like—"

"They never found her body, but they found her blood, lots of it. Our bodies only hold eight pints of the stuff. She bled out on that church floor." He sighs. "She's dead, Gina, believe me."

"She used to cut herself and then watch the blood drip out of her, let it pour into cups and bottles and shit. Maybe she saved it." I can see her slowly running a knife over her belly, telling me the pain made her feel alive. I can see her lowering her blouse over her shoulders, revealing scars. "She did it for years. Could be—"

"You think your sister was that insane?" He waves his hand as though he's dismissing me.

"Yes. Yes, I do."

Daniel does not respond. He's lost in thought as I pour hot water into a mug and then add a teabag. It's as though there's a wall around him, as though he's shut the rest of the world out. I put his tea before him and he stares into the brown liquid. Does he see things there? I turn away and pour coffee for myself, add sugar and milk. I drink in silence.

The house is quiet. The streets are silent. I sit across from Daniel. He's still staring into his cup. Where has he gone? Back to the evidence? Is it replaying it through his mind? Could Allie have set up Rico? I'm not sorry I told Daniel what Allie did with her blood. I'm not sorry I believe in her insanity, in her abilities to conjure up evil or even the dead.

I wish the storm would end. I wish they'd all end.

18

I wash the cups and put them away. Daniel hasn't spoken a word since we discussed my sister's insanity, the possibility she was involved in murders and that she could still be alive. He remained deep in thought, drinking his tea. Later, he went to the living room, book beneath his arm, eyeglasses at the tip of his nose.

I wish he'd cough, call out to me, but I only hear book pages turning every few minutes and the sound of his body shifting in the chair. I shut the cupboard door, turn off the faucet and listen to the pipes groan. I decide to see if Daniel still wants to go downstairs with me. I need to break the silence. After putting away the dish towel I make my way to the living room to find him deeply absorbed in his book. He runs his hand through his hair and turns another page. I clear my throat. "Still going with me?"

He checks his watch. "Yeah, didn't realize how late it was. Good book." He lays it on the armrest, stands, then follows me to the door.

I open the door, peer into the hallway and listen. "Building's quiet."

"Heard somebody come up the stairs and go into an apartment down the hall. Can't believe people were out in this."

"Dave Sousa," I tell him. "He's the only other one on this floor, works in my office. That job is his life. He's an asshole, takes pleasure in humiliating subordinates in front of others. I had a run-in with him last week." I can see Dave waving his finger at me and smirking playfully, his front teeth protruding over his lips. "Hey, I'm still learning. A lot of my day job is trial and error. I told him to fuck off."

Daniel laughs lightly. "I know the type. They're usually the guys who got picked on in high school. Now they think they know it all. They feel good about themselves by making others feel small."

"He probably walked home in the snow. Cheap bastard wouldn't ever pay for car service or even a bus. I can almost see him trudging down Broadway with that stupid look he always has on his face."

"Give him the benefit of the doubt. Nothing's probably running tonight, he might not have had any choice but to walk."

"I'm surprised he didn't spend the night at the office sleeping with his file cabinet. They're *very* close."

Daniel laughs harder this time but tries to keep the volume low as we pass Dave's apartment. All I hear is the quiet hum of a TV. Dave's boots are against his door and puddles of water have formed beneath them.

We make our way down the stairs in a silence that quickly becomes unsettling. Why isn't Frankie's girlfriend singing? Why aren't pots and pans banging in old lady Tilton's apartment?

"How many people live in this building?" Daniel asks.

"A tenant just passed away, so right now only Frankie the super and his girlfriend, Mrs. Tilton and Dave. There are two empty studios and a couple empty apartments going up for rent. Super said the owner's cleaning them up, fixing stuff. Frankie's doing most of the work, painting, sanding the floors, plumbing and all that. Top floors are closed off. No one ever lives there."

We reach the bottom of the stairs. The front door is open and snow is barreling in from outside. "Where the fuck is Frankie? He wouldn't leave the door open like that."

His apartment door is shut. It's normally open at least a crack so he can see who comes in and out, so he can air out the place when his girlfriend cooks up her concoctions. "We should check." Daniel moves his hand over his jacket, and though he doesn't draw his weapon, he finds the slight bulge his holster causes and pats it as if to be sure it's still there. "Why don't you knock, ask if they're ok?"

I rap lightly on the door. "You in there, guys? Just checking you're OK, storm and all, you know."

Silence.

I knock again, harder this time, and the door opens slightly. "You guys OK?" Something's wrong. I feel it in my gut.

I sense Daniel has the same feeling as he gently pushes me aside blocking my view as he pushes the door open.

"Gina, go upstairs."

"What's wrong?" I move up behind Daniel and before he can stop me I'm standing beside him. I see Frankie sprawled on the floor. His throat has been slashed. His blood is so red, so wet on the dark wooden floor. Lilly is curled up in a corner. She's shaking violently and weeping. She's holding a knife in her hand. "Spells couldn't save him. I couldn't bring him back, couldn't do nothing," she babbles. A pot boils on the stove.

"What happened, Miss?" Daniel moves towards her. His hand is on his holster.

Lilly shakes her head back and forth. "Couldn't make it work. You gonna arrest me, officer? I didn't do it. I swear. I went to my sister's a few blocks away, spent a few hours there. Went to the liquor store, but it wasn't open. Nothings open in this fucking city—"

"Gina, that you?" Someone calls from the top of the stairs. I turn and move towards the door. Dave is standing there awkwardly. Blood spurts from his chest as a dark figure moves up behind him. It spreads elongated fingers and presses them against Dave's back. "Gina, old lady Tilton is all cut up—" Dave puts both hands on his chest as if to stop the explosion of blood but it runs between his fingers. "Run," he says, gagging, then he falls down the stairs, tumbling like a broken marionette, the bones in his legs and arms snapping and breaking with each violent roll. A shower of blood explodes when he hits the bottom step, spraying the hallway and walls, creating crimson patterns like spidery legs and twisted tree limbs. I move toward him, hypnotized or perhaps still unable to quite grasp what I've just seen.

Daniel yells. "Gina, don't move. I'm calling for backup. Just stay put. Don't touch anything." Daniel talks fast, the words coming out in a rapid-fire cadence. He deftly handcuffs Lilly to a radiator with his free hand and then draws his weapon.

I feel like I'm going to faint. Lilly is still babbling. Snow piles up at the door. Daniel curses then shakes his head as he puts his cell to his ear. My instinct is to run, to get away from here, but there's nowhere to go. I wish the snow would clear so I could leave this city, all the death, all the lunacy, all the pain. But I can't. The snow keeps coming, locking us all in tight, holding us here like prisoners.

19

"Phone's out, can't get through. Shit. Let's get upstairs. Maybe we'll have better luck with your landline. This whole fucking building is a crime scene, try not to touch the banisters and don't step in the blood, it'll taint the evidence. We've got to preserve as much of it as we can." Daniel wraps his arm around me. "Just move with me, don't be afraid." His voice is shaky. He's being strong for me, but I know he's afraid too.

We move past Dave. His fingers are still twitching, his eyes are glazed over and blood seeps from dozens of wounds on his neck and chest. I didn't like the guy, but never wished him dead, never wanted to see him this way. Guilt fills me as I think of all the times I wished bad things for him, how I'd once visualized a cab hitting him as he jaywalked across a block, or how I imagined him falling off a platform as a subway blasted down the tracks. I never meant any of it.

"Poor bastard was dead before he hit the landing." Daniel looks to a deep wound in Dave's neck. "Don't look. I've got you. You're shivering."

"The killer could be—"

"Don't think, just walk." Daniel listens as the house settles, as if it speaks to him with its subtle creaks. "Just walk." We begin our ascent up the stairs. Daniel wraps one arm tighter around me, his hand gently rubbing against my shoulder. The other clutches his gun. He looks to both sides then above us. Slowly, he turns and looks behind us. "Keep moving, kid." He maneuvers me around a puddle of blood. The wind howls and fast falling snow pummels the old building. The lights repeatedly flicker on and off as we continue upward.

When we reach my door, it's still ajar. Daniel disentangles himself from me, puts a finger to his lip and whispers, "Don't move. Stay in the shadows and scream your fucking head off if you see anyone." He quietly moves ahead of me, turns and levels his gun in front of him. He looks from left to right.

I stand near a lopsided coat rack, hopefully blending with the jagged shadows it casts. I wait as Daniel moves through the rooms, probably peering beneath furniture, looking behind open doors and curtains. I swear I hear heavy breathing beneath me, footsteps slowly climbing the stairs. Boots thump twice then stop. Soft, menacing laughter erupts from the second-floor landing.

Below, Lilly lets out a blood-curdling scream.

The lights go out. This time they don't come back on. "Daniel!" I whisper to myself, to the walls and to the darkness around. No answer comes. I move against the wall, try to make myself invisible. I don't want to die here in darkness. "Daniel," my voice is lost within the sounds and fury of the storm. I'll be swallowed up alive by it, by this tumultuous night and by the evil lurking somewhere in this building.

Finally, Daniel appears at the door. "Gina, don't speak. Come quick, it's ok, come on inside. It's safe in here."

I let out a deep sigh of relief as Daniel takes my hand, pulls me inside then bolts the door behind us. "No lights, no nothing, I heard something downstairs, I heard a voice, I—we'll never get out of here alive, we'll never—"

"It'll be OK." He grabs my shoulders firmly and looks me in the eye. "Gina, look at me. It'll be OK. You got to hold it together, you hear me?"

I nod and try to stay in control, but in my mind I'm still pleading with him to get us out of here, my voice coming from a place I don't know, a place of fear and death.

"We've got to lay low. You got candles, a kerosene lamp or something?"

"Yeah, there are candles on the bookshelf, matches beside the big one shaped like a cat. I love that candle. It was a gift from Allie, I never lit it, I always wanted to preserve it along with the others, wax objects in the shapes of stars, moons and assorted small animals, I—"

"Easy," he says, "it's OK. Deep breaths, Gina, deep breaths."

I somehow stop the flow of words tumbling from my mouth as Daniel strikes a match, lights the beautiful cat candle and then a crescent moon splashed with glitter next to it.

"I heard Lilly. I think she was screaming." I tell him. "But maybe I'm wrong. I wish she'd do something—I wish she'd sing. I wish she'd chant like she used to."

"I locked the door behind her. She's as safe as we are right now if that's any consolation. I've got to get back down there. Check out the rest of the house. If I can I've got to try to bring Lilly back here with us." He removes his cell phone from his pocket, punches in numbers and then listens. "Shit, still not working." He puts the phone back in his pocket. "I doubt Lilly's behind all this, but you never know. I'll keep trying the phones. Your landline is out too, tried it while I was checking the place out. Either the storm knocked down lines or somebody cut them. Either way, they're of no use to us now. What a surprise. I need to get the building secured as best I can."

"I'll go with you."

"No, you stay here, keep trying your phone. If you've got a cell phone try that too, you might get lucky and get a signal, they come in and out in weather like this."

"Who the hell is doing this?"

"When the storm's over we'll know the truth." He looks to the bookcase as if he notices something odd. "Funny."

"What?"

"I don't remember putting that book back." Daniel grabs a book from the shelf, holds it by the binding. The pages fan out and something falls free. He bends down and picks up one of Allie's miniature paintings.

"It was Allie's," I tell Daniel. "She called them Artist's trading cards, used to sell them on eBay. She told me it was the latest rage. I'm not sure how it got inside that book, though."

"Odd piece." He studies it in the palm of one hand but holds it so I can see that it's a collage with strange magical symbols and torn, yellowed pages of text. He points to an odd-shaped pattern. "These odd shapes, Allie must have studied them, known a lot about them. She's painted them in all four corners. I've seen them used before. These are signatures, supposedly of beings—and people—who serve the Devil, but she's made crosses over them. Paper she used is old, looks like it came from an old journal or some kind of handmade book. Symbol in the middle, the rose, along with the crosses, supposedly keeps everything hidden from the Devil." He continues to stare at the little painting in his left hand. In his other hand he clutches the book, his thumb holding it open to a page of photographs. The stills are a series featuring black men and women, sepia-toned, vintage. One subject stands out, his eyes dark and haunting, his suit and hat strangely familiar. It's the demon I've seen in bars, in subways, standing next to the beautiful woman in the church in Harlem.

"Who's that?" I ask Daniel, pointing to the photograph. He gently places Allie's artwork on a stack of books on the shelf then studies the photo. "Mojo DeCanne," he says quietly, almost hesitantly. "The legendary evil one from Harlem, the founder of the church where they found Allie's—"

"I've seen him before."

"Yeah, he's in a lot of these books on magic. The old bookstores on Fourth Avenue always had them. They had an entire section about him at *Samuel Wisner's Occult and all Subjects Bookstore* back in the day. I had an elderly aunt who had an entire collection she'd bought there. She used to call them Manhattan Grimoires. DeCanne—you must have seen his picture in one place or another in this city."

"No," I tell him, swallowing with some difficulty. "Daniel, I've *really* seen him."

"You imagined it. You probably saw a photo and dreamed about him."

"No, you don't understand."

"He's dead, Gina, long dead." He waves his hand. "How about opening some of the canned goods you're saving? Got gas or electric cooking?"

"Gas."

"Good, we can have hot soup when I get back, OK?" He smiles, obviously trying to relax me in the midst of this dizzying madness. He puts the book atop the art then winks at me. "Go ahead and start on it, it'll keep your mind focused on something."

I'm not hungry. Mojo DeCanne is haunting me. He's come back

from the dead, maybe he never died at all and he's after me—just like he was after Allie. I know it in my gut and I'm so afraid he's in this house, afraid he'll burst in here any minute and kill both of us. No matter how adept Daniel is with a gun, no matter how much of a skilled fighter he is, he can't defend us against bad magic, against evil both ancient and potent.

"Listen to me," he says firmly. "You'll be OK."

He holds my stare until I offer a slight nod, then moves to the door.

Before his hand reaches the knob, something thumps against it.

Despite the candlelight it somehow suddenly seems darker than before. I think about how Daniel once told me there are things in this city that can never be explained, and I notice him looking at me again, his eyes intense now and laced with fear as another thump erupts against the door. I know he's thinking the same thing I am, and despite his attempted façade, despite his apparent disregard for what I've just told him, I can tell he understands we're dealing with something beyond that which we can fully understand.

I watch as he draws his weapon with one hand then pulls the door open wide with the other, his gun panning back and forth across the darkness. Whoever or whatever was thumping against the door has retreated.

"Bolt the door behind me," he whispers without looking at me. "It'll be all right, just do what I say."

He steps into the darkness carefully, gun leveled in front of him and leading the way. Holding a stance, he moves forward with stealth and skill years of training has made second nature to him. I latch the door and secure all the chain locks then listen as Daniel's footsteps move down the hallway and eventually become soft patter on the stairs.

Be strong, I tell myself. Control your nerves.

A voice in my head whispers: *What if he doesn't come back?*

I go to the kitchen. But for wavering candle flames, the room is dark. Yellow and orange tongues of fire dance above a wax cat head, hypnotic and alluring. My sister once told me that witches can cast spells while looking into the flickering light of a candle and sometimes visions materialize where the past and the future play out like a movie if they stare hard enough.

My sister told me lots of crazy things.

The cat's face starts to melt as wax drips across his almond-shaped eyes and obliterates his whiskers.

"Gina?"

This time the voice isn't in my head, and even as my mind feels like it's coming apart, I know exactly whose voice it is.

I turn. Allie is sitting at the kitchen table, a knife in her hand.

20

Despite my fear I move closer until I can see her face clearly. There are deep cuts in her skin, entire pieces of flesh scooped away and puddles of crimson on the table. Blood drips slowly from the knife blade in her hand.

"Allie." Her name escapes me as a quiet gasp.

"I'm imperfect," she says through ruined lips. "Mojo said I needed to be remade, needed to cut away what's ugly, what's soiled." She raises the knife to her right eye and begins to carve away at the lid.

"Allie, *stop.*"

But she's not listening. A fresh piece of flesh falls like spiraling ribbon to the table. She smiles. "Don't give Mojo the art I made. It's not his. If you do I'll never be beautiful again." She licks blood from her chin. "I'll never be beautiful again."

"Allie, what the fuck is happening?" I feel lightheaded, rub my eyes quickly.

And then she's gone. The room is empty. No Allie, no blood, no knife.

Just as I've become convinced I've completely lost my mind, I hear an unsettling noise that sounds like a snake hissing.

A dark shadow crawls across the floor, and for a moment I see the face of Mojo DeCanne glaring back at me from the darkness on the far side of the room. Demon lips speak, but words come from another world, from someplace evil and forsaken. "Give me what's mine, bitch." Laughter breaks out. "I carved up your boyfriend. He's down in the basement in a thousand pieces." The shadowy thing stands, waves an elongated finger then extends its hand, turning the palm upward. A vision of Daniel appears, lying there with his throat cut, his fingers strewn across the floor and his intestines falling from his belly.

The demon whispers something else but it comes out as an indecipherable hiss. As the pitch rises and intensifies, I slide to the floor, cover my ears and close my eyes. Insane or damned, it hardly seems to matter now.

And then there's a pounding sound. Hard and fast, it's comes from the living room or maybe the bedroom. It continues, harder and faster.

"Gina, open the fucking window!"

A muffled voice, but one I recognize as Daniel's. He's alive, thank God, he's alive. I get up and quickly look around the kitchen. I'm alone.

I run to the living room and find Daniel standing on the fire escape still pounding on the window. I open it, tearing a nail on the latch.

He climbs in. Snow covers his clothes and his hair. "I've been knocking for five minutes. Where the hell were you?"

"I was scared."

"You can get frostbite real quick in this weather. Christ, I'm freezing." He pulls the window shut, locks it then speaks rapidly. "Look, I checked the whole house. Nobody's alive. Not even Lilly. Someone got to her, windows were all open. We gotta make sure all of yours are locked." He treks through my apartment with me following. "I didn't see anyone. They could be hiding. Maybe they left, I don't know. I checked outside as best I could. There's blood all over the walk, down in the alley. It's fucking blinding out there and nobody's around. We wouldn't get fifty feet on foot out there in this mess. I tried my phone again too. Nothing."

"I tried too," I tell him. "My cell. I can't remember where—"

"Everything's out. City's crippled, you don't see storms this bad more than a couple times a century."

"Lilly…how…"

"You don't need to know."

"I heard him. He called to me. I know it sounds insane, like I'm some crazy fucking bag lady or something, but I'm telling you I heard him."

"Heard who?"

"Mojo DeCanne."

His expression fails to hide his annoyance. "Gina, get it together, come on. Whoever did all this is alive, a person from this century, not some dead sorcerer. We've got enough real shit to worry about, OK? There are dead bodies all over the building."

"You know it's him. You can feel it. I know you can."

"I'm a cop. I can't let my imagination run away with me. Not now."

"You feel the evil the same as I do. You heard the thumping on the door just like I did."

"Mojo DeCanne is dead."

"Maybe we are too."

He doesn't say a word, just wraps his arms around me and we stand there in silence. I can feel his heart pounding and our bodies trembling.

If we stay like this forever it'll be all right, I tell myself. If only we could stay this way until whatever is out there comes to claim us then at least our last moments would have been worthwhile.

21

If things were normal, we'd be lovers by now. We would have tasted each other from head to foot, known intimate secrets of flesh and carnal ecstasy and felt the connection of two souls becoming one. But nothing is normal. Daniel and I exist inside a tomb sealed with ice and snow, side by side with the dead.

I hold my sister's miniature painting, study the color, form, text and odd symbols. Daniel sits on the couch, a small taper candle burning on the table by his side, the book containing Mojo DeCanne's photograph in his lap. "Gina," he says, "bring the art here, I want to show you something." His voice is tired, his movements slow.

I do as he asks, and sit beside him. Gently, he lifts the art from my palm and lays it side by side with another photograph of Mojo DeCanne, the man with devil eyes and deadly incantations tattooed on his soul. Daniel moves his index finger from book to painting as he speaks. "See? Mojo's ceremonial robe has the same markings as the signatures on Allie's art. She must have studied about him. The text must be from one old book or another, probably one she found in the basement of The Strand or something she bought on a street corner. Makes sense, no?"

"Nothing makes sense."

Allie's words ring in my head.

Don't give Mojo the art I made. It's not his. If you do I'll never be beautiful again.

Daniel doesn't answer me. He turns a page, finds another picture of Mojo. A young white man stands next to him and they're shaking hands, smiling. An array of strange African masks hangs on a wall behind them, and both men wear turn of the century clothing. The other man is someone I recognize immediately, the man who I've lived with for months and the man who left me without a word a night ago. Or was it two nights ago now—a lifetime maybe—time seems to be losing all meaning in the storm.

"Tony," I say in a tiny voice.

"Anthony Marandacci, son of a don from back in the day. He studied with DeCanne, defied his father. The Mojo man supposedly took him under his wing and taught him all his darkest secrets. Marandacci was a punk nonetheless, and he was killed in a bar fight. People say his own father's people got to him. Story goes DeCanne captured Anthony's soul with some heebie-jeebie before he took up permanent residence in Hell. People say sometimes Anthony and DeCanne still work together as a team from the beyond."

"It can't be. Tony was my boyfriend. I thought I loved him."

"What?"

"Tony," I tell him again, the sound of his name strange on my tongue, "I know him. He lived with me up until—"

"What the fuck, Gina? This guy's dead. They're both dead. All the stories are bogus, they're stupid Halloween stories designed to scare kids."

"He lived with me until a few days ago," I tell him evenly. "I'm not lying to you, Daniel."

He sighs heavily. "I'm not saying you're lying."

"He still holds a key in all this." My eyes dart to the door. The deadbolts are fastened, but can't bad magic break through bolted doors?

Daniel lays the book at his side. "Look, my Grandma believed, OK? I grew up listening to her, but once I got out of the house, got to college then joined the force I took what she said with a grain of salt. I held her hand as she died, you know. She told me she saw good things around me, but one day evil would challenge me." He thinks for a moment then waves his hand. "I loved her, and she meant well, but it's all crazy superstition."

"Stop lying to yourself. You believed once and this whole thing is making you remember what your Grandmother taught you. I know it. I feel it."

He waves his hand again, as if to knock my words from the air. "Get some sleep. I'll stay up until morning, keep trying the phones. Something's got to give by first light."

I lay my head on his shoulder without speaking, and he puts his arm around me.

I fall asleep dreaming of Allie.

She sits on her bed like she did as a child, surrounded by paper and paint. She works feverishly, as if fearful lightning might strike her at any moment and rob her of the opportunity to leave some piece of her soul behind.

"I touch God when I do this," she says without looking at me, focused instead on a miniature piece of art she's working on. "It's the only time I feel good."

I watch as her fingers and hands move rapidly.

"I've pasted Mojo's words on watercolor paper," she tells me. "It's the only way you'll figure it out."

Yellowed pages materialize and float above her head. When I return my gaze to her, I notice blood on her bed sheet.

Realizing I've seen it, she gazes up at me. "When Mojo fucks me he makes me bleed. Sometimes it lasts for days."

I stare at her numbly.

"We met at a dump on the lower West Side last time I saw him," she says. "We fucked for hours with the curtains wide open so people in the next building could see. He left me there, didn't even kiss me goodbye. The blood wouldn't stop that night. It hurt so bad between my legs I thought I was going to die that night, alone in a whore hotel with roaches crawling up the walls, with a grimy desk clerk blasting his radio so loud the sound carried up three flights. I never knew what real loneliness was until then. Then I thought about all the people who die in this city every day, alone and forgotten, and realized they knew what it was too."

"You should have called me," I tell her.

"No, the demons in the lobby would have stopped you. I had to wait until dawn, until they went back to their hole under the bridge. Mojo's followers look out for shit like that, you know."

I'm about to ask her more about it when a gush of blood pours from between her legs. "Jesus, Allie, you're bleeding, you..."

She glances down as if mildly annoyed. "It stings," she says flatly. "I swear, it feels like he did me with a knife. But he's just an animal, a devil back from the dead."

"Allie, come home to me."

"Can't, gotta keep moving. And so do you. He's coming for you."

"Why Allie, why is he coming for me? What does he want with me?"

"I left his secret with you." She begins to cry and paint with her own blood, strange symbols, portraits of Tony and Mojo in a dark city.

"Tony's one of his followers, isn't he?" I ask softly.

She nods. "At least he didn't make you bleed. At least he spared you that."

"I'm so sorry, I—Allie, what do I do, how do I stop DeCanne?"

"You're the only one—" Blood spurts from her mouth, runs out over her bottom lip and she gags, coughs, spraying even more onto the bed. "This is a dream," she says, eyes sad and distant now, voice gurgling with blood. "*I'm* a dream."

The snow comes down hard. I stand there helplessly and watch as it buries my sister, silencing her.

As the curtains of snow part, I find myself on the corner of West Broadway and Prince.

A dark figure comes toward me, his black cape spread out behind him like wings. Footsteps echo on the city walk and Mojo's dead face is suddenly illuminated, gleaming beneath a street lamp. "Give me back my spell, bitch." His voice sounds as if he's swallowed broken glass. "You think you've seen slaughter, you think you've seen death? I'll bring you straight to Hell. Give it back!"

His hand reaches for me and I am jolted awake as pipes rattle in the apartment.

Daniel, still next to me, sighs deeply. "Sleep, girl," he whispers.

I drift away. Maybe I was never fully awake, I can't be sure, but in my dreams, I hear snow pummeling windows, wind rattling glass and the house creaking and settling against the wind's constant assault. I hear Daniel breathe again and feel him shift position as his arm tightens around me, and I wonder if in dreams we're all dead and trapped in Mojo DeCanne's never-ending Hell.

22

It's still dark. All is silent but for the groans of the old building. It's a pre-war structure, with high ceilings, large rooms, hardwood floors, crown moldings and thick firewalls between apartments, one of many in this city, built before World War II. Lots of people consider buildings like this charming, but it gets creepy sometimes. Noises, strange smells and odd shadows are abundant. Only the first three floors are occupied. Frankie told me the other floors were closed, cordoned off a dozen years ago. He said he wasn't allowed up there and it's a mystery why, only the owner knows the secret. The rental agreement here was a steal and I never quite understood why the mysterious owner chose to keep most of the building empty and to charge such low rent.

I came upon this place quite by accident. I was searching the Internet for Manhattan rentals, never thinking I could find a place I could afford, when I happened upon a website called Decker Rentals. This was the only building advertised. The ad said the building was "in need of special tenants." Twelve-fifty for a large bedroom, kitchen, living room, bath and studio is a phenomenal price in lower Manhattan, and I figured it was just a huge come-on, but I entered my email address and phone number and waited to see what happened.

By the following day I had an appointment to see the place. Expecting to be contacted by a smooth-talking mob type with slicked-back hair and a gold chip in his front tooth, I instead met with an agent named Tressie Manetti, a tall redhead with long curling fingernails, a penchant for smoking extra-long cigarettes and a large smile. And rather than a rundown, rat-infested dump that stunk to high heaven, I was surprised to find a really nice space I could see myself living in. After Tressie had shown me the place, I asked her what the catch was. "Is there running water? Does the plumbing work? Do drug dealers live next door? What's the problem? Come on, there has to be one."

She lit a cigarette, took a drag and flicked the ashes as if she were outside, "Look, it's in the contract." She pointed to bold black print. "If after a month you are not totally satisfied, your security deposit and last month's rent will be returned. If after a month you're satisfied then your lease will be activated. So, sign on the dotted line or show this to a lawyer first, your choice." She smiled at me. I think her teeth were false, and up close, she looked a lot older than she initially appeared.

Though still a bit suspicious, I signed. The place was listed with The American Association of Realtors. There are laws after all. Within days I was satisfied that the water ran properly, the plumbing worked and there were no drug dealers in the vicinity, but I never saw Tressie Manetti again. I gave my rent check to Frankie every month and he deposited it into the owner's account. No strings. No problems except for the creaks, noisy pipes, meeting Dave on the stairs and hearing Lilly curse.

Now only the creaks and noisy pipes are left.

"Gina, I boiled some hot water on the stove, made some instant coffee, tea if you like, and a couple of eggs. Come into the kitchen."

Daniel's voice brings me back from my memories, but I'm still wondering what happened to Tressie and who is going to let the owner of this place know what's happened here, that the super and some of the tenants have been murdered.

"Gina? Come on." Daniel stands in the hall, hands on hips. "Snow hasn't let up much at all. The phones are still out and morning's about to break." He hesitates a moment. "Did a lot of reading last night, uncovered some interesting stuff."

"Like what?" I say rubbing my eyes.

"This house, did you know the DeCanne family once owned it?"

"No, I—of course not—God no, I had no idea." My heart sinks. "But I was just thinking about how I first found this place."

He shakes his finger back and forth. "I just meant it's interesting that you're living here, OK? Don't go getting all creepy on me again."

"Oh, right, sorry. My neighbors have all been slaughtered

overnight and we're trapped here and I'm seeing things and experiencing things that can't be, what was I thinking? How could I be so silly as to get *creepy* on you again?"

"Gina, relax."

"Relax?" I laugh, but am anything but amused. It spills out of me uncontrollably. "Sure, right away."

"The DeCanne family is dead. All of them, dead, understand? They can't hurt you. Some big real estate tycoon probably has his hands on the building now. I'll get to the bottom of all this, I'll find out what's happened here, but—"

"No, you don't know how I found this place."

"Look, it's all just coincidence. Weird, OK, I agree, but coincidence."

"It all fits together now. DeCanne was setting me up in case Allie split on him and—"

"Gina, don't start. It's been a horrific night for both of us, enough with your voodoo stories."

I hear deep eerie laughter erupt from below—laughter only I can hear—and I wonder what it's going to take to convince Daniel that this place could be Hell and that Mojo DeCanne is coming for us. Daniel knows this place has been turned into a house of horrors but he thinks it's just another legitimate crime scene and that once his forensic buddies get here things will be explained and logically sorted out. He thinks life will go back to normal, or as normal as it gets in a cop's life, once this storm has passed. He's wrong. He's been wrong before and he's wrong now. The Devil delights in non-believers, preys on those with dismissive natures.

The laughter sounds again and fear consumes me like never before.

23

It seems as though this snow is never going to stop and New York will become a world forever covered in white, forever lost, cut off and out of touch with the rest of the world, a new Atlantis, gone but not quite forgotten, its inhabitants and legacy the stuff of legend and mystery.

Daniel's face is drawn, eyes red. He stretches and yawns as I think about the empty floors in the building and how demons and dark angels could inhabit the damp and dusty apartments below.

"Daniel, did you check out the fourth and fifth floors? Someone—something—could be hiding there."

He nods. "There's a steel gate on the fourth-floor landing. It's bolted in three places. Nobody can get under it or over it. If they gained entry by a fire escape and climbed in a window they wouldn't be able to get downstairs. Don't worry."

"But if it's something supernatural, if it's someone with magical power."

He rolls his eyes. "Well then, I guess there's nothing we can do about it, right? Come on, Gina, let's not go there again."

"We have to go there. You have to open your mind and remember the things your grandmother told you, the things you forgot when you left home."

"Look, I'm beat. We'll talk about it after I've slept a few hours. We're locked in and locked down, no one's getting in here. Long as we stay put we're safe. You gonna be OK if I nod off?"

"I can take care of myself."

He smiles. "Sure. Wake me if anything happens. Unless Dracula suddenly appears, let me sleep."

"He can't right now," I say with a smirk, "it's daytime."

"We'll talk when I wake up. Is the couch comfortable?"

"If you want to use my bed it's fine. The sheets were washed day before yesterday and there's plenty of blankets." I think of how I shared that bed with Tony, with a phantom, with Mojo DeCanne's disciple. Was Mojo laughing, watching, when Tony and I were together? Did he peer at us from a dark corner, from behind the drapes?

"Thanks." Daniel walks slowly towards me, stops in front of me and kisses me gently on the lips. He looks at me almost shyly then backs away, turns and disappears down the hall.

I watch the snow, still falling steadily, swirling and drifting. I take a seat on the window ledge and reach for a cup of coffee. I must have left it there last night. Maybe it's been here for days, I'm not sure. I lift it and smell the strong aroma. It's lukewarm. Not bad.

"Gina." A soft voice calls from below. I see something dark moving within the thick snow, a black splotch amidst the endless whiteout. You're exhausted, I tell myself, maybe you're still asleep and dreaming, still snuggled close to Daniel on the couch.

But I can feel it. I can feel *him*. He's coming. Mojo DeCanne.

A gust of wind parts the snow long enough for me to glimpse him standing there, dressed in a turn of the century suit. His wide-brimmed hat covers his eyes. He raises a crooked finger and wags it back and forth at me in a scolding motion. After a moment, his tongue slowly protrudes from his mouth, catching snowflakes with it like a child might. His tongue drips with blood, which stains the snow, then seems to grow longer, extending a few inches before I hear his laughter. With his snake-like tongue shimmering and slick with ice and crimson, he walks closer to the building with a long, eerie gait, until I am no longer able to see him from my vantage point.

But I can still hear him.

The door down in the lobby sounds as it opens then closes.

Footsteps, slow and deliberate, plod up the stairs…one by one.

"Gina." His voice is childlike but horrifying all at once. "Gina," he says again, only this time it's the voice of a demon.

Trembling uncontrollably, I move toward the door and look into the peephole.

He's crouched over, his tongue lapping the hole. As I stagger back I scream, "Daniel! Daniel!" And yet my voice sounds so small, as if I barely made any sound at all. The door rattles. The knob turns. Something comes through the keyhole, pink, wet and serpent-like, and I can hear him laughing again, his breath heavy and gurgling on the other side of the thin door that separates us. The tongue spirals towards me, curling, seeming to reach for me, wanting to wrap itself around my neck.

Something coils around my throat, thick and wet as it tightens and chokes me, pulls me down into a cold and never-ending darkness.

"Daniel!"

I feel sudden pressure on my shoulders, and the sensation of being shaken. "Gina! Wake up!"

The darkness becomes light, and I see Daniel standing before me. "What the fuck, Gina? Are you sleepwalking now?"

As things come back into focus and my mind processes what's happened, I turn away, look back at the door. It stands closed, locked, undisturbed. "He was here. He tried to get inside. His fucking tongue was coming through the keyhole, it—it touched me. My face, it—look, my face is still wet."

He touches my cheek. "You're crying. Don't you know that you're crying?"

I hesitantly touch my face with shaking hands. He's right. Tears. I'm crying and I didn't even realize it. "But I saw him," I say quietly. "Daniel, I *felt* him."

"Mojo DeCanne?" he asks.

I nod.

"Look, girl, you've got to get that shit out of your head. Once that sort of thing gets into your mind it's hard to shake, you understand?"

"Oh really, is that so? I thought it was all bullshit."

"It is," he says evenly. "Unless you choose to believe in it, then like anything else, it has power, power you gave it."

"Why can't you just believe me?"

"Come lie down with me. Get Mojo out of your head, I'm tired of talking about it."

If it were any other time I'd melt at the thought of sleeping beside Daniel, but not now.

"Stop treating me like a little girl, like I'm crazy."

"Look, we've both been through one hell of an ordeal, and we're exhausted, not thinking straight. Just lie down with me for a while. We'll talk more after we get some rest, OK?"

I stare at him defiantly for a long time before I finally give in and allow him to lead me to the bedroom. I lie down first, wait for him to pull the covers up over me. Then he lies down next to me, wraps his arms around me and holds me tight. I feel about as safe as I can, considering, but I know in my gut all hell is breaking loose around us. I heard Mojo's laughter, laughter he allows only me to hear, and I wonder how long he'll torment me like this before he grows bored and tries to destroy me completely.

24

Daniel's breath is soft in my ear. He mumbles something in his sleep. I wonder if Mojo DeCanne speaks to him in dreams, comes to him disguised as a perp wearing clothes stained with his last victim's blood. Daniel's hold on me loosens as he shifts in his sleep. More unintelligible words escape from his lips.

I can't fall asleep, not now. So, I'll just listen to Daniel's dreamtime sighs and words whispered to beings that reside in his subconscious. The window in the bedroom rattles as a gust of wind strikes hard. A cracking noise erupts. A minute or two later, it happens again. I slip out of bed, afraid that perhaps a buildup of ice has cracked one of the windowpanes. Two windows cracked last winter during a cold spell and I heard that noise before it happened. But when I reach the window, there's no damage.

With sleep no longer an option at this point, I move into the living room and perch on the window ledge, holding my breath for a moment, and pray Mojo DeCanne isn't standing in the alley. He isn't. Instead I see the woman from my dreams making her way up the fire escape. She's wearing a black velvet shawl and a long vintage dress. Her hair falls in thick dark braids down her back. She sees me and smiles. She slips and I fear she'll tumble down the stairs, but she regains her balance just in time then continues to climb upward. A warm, safe feeling engulfs me as I unlatch the window, wait for her to complete her ascent then watch her lift her dress, hook one leg over the ledge and climb inside.

"The Devil's out there," she says, brushing snow from her clothes and shaking her head. Bells tied within hair ribbons jingle, and her bracelets click. "Colder than I ever remember."

Isn't this woman supposed to be dead, an apparition? Or is this someone else, someone I've seen, someone that's following me, someone that's mad as I am? "Who are you?"

She smiles. Bells chime. "Anna DeCanne."

My heart pounds. "DeCanne?"

She leans forward as though she's about to bow, and I detect the scent of flowers, roses and lilies. "My son," she says, "you fear my son. I brought good magic with me to this country, but he twisted it."

"This is another dream, isn't it?"

"Perceive it as you like. I've been trying to tell you things, but you're allowing the dark things—him—to invade your thoughts and feelings." She holds out her hand. "Come with me, be quick and don't think of him. I promise you'll be safe if you stay close and listen." She moves back toward the window, raises one leg over the ledge and then the other. "Take my hand."

I give her my hand and she gently pulls me over the ledge. She holds on tightly as we climb the fire escape, and then I wait as she raises a window on the fourth-floor landing. She eases herself inside, helps me into an empty room. "Keep your windows locked," she urges. "If I can find my way down then so can others." She kneels on the floor, lifts a board then removes a box and begins to rummage through it. Eventually she removes a book, torn and shabby. "Your sister stole Mojo's most potent spell, put it in one of her artsy creations. He's still chasing her, trying to get it back, through the veils of life, death and back, they go round and round."

"I'll give it back. Will he stop? Will he leave us all alone if I give it back?"

"It's not that easy."

I shrug. "Nothing ever is, is it?"

"He brings the dead back with that spell, brought lots of us back already. No telling who or what he'll infect the good Earth with if he gets it in his hands again."

"Allie, she—"

"She did it on her own, came back on her own power." Anna shakes her head. "Smart kid, but doomed."

"What do I do?"

She hands me Mojo's book. "Use the spell of reversal. It'll work. You can do it. You're Allie's blood."

"Spell of fucking what?"

Footsteps sound in the hall. "I have to go. Go home. I'll see you again."

"No, wait. I don't know what to do."

Ignoring me, she stands and exits through a splintered door. The footsteps grow louder but I'm frozen in place even as the doorknob turns.

And then he's standing there, blood trickling from his lips. Eyes filled with hate. DeCanne holds a knife, something ancient and wicked, and begins to laugh. "It's a dream, little Gina. Once you wake, the book will disappear. I promise. You believe in my promises, don't you, bitch?" I remember my mother kneeling on the floor, screaming at the top of her lungs, telling her demons to go away and I say. "Go away, just leave me be. You're not real." He takes a step closer. "You have something of mine. I can take it whenever I choose, but I like playing with you, seeing you shiver."

"You're not real."

"Believe in me, and I can take death away. Don't you want to walk with me forever, Gina?"

"Fuck you."

He laughs, loud and chilling. "You *do* believe in me. You know you do."

"Go to Hell," I whisper, his breath on my face, his cold fingers touching me.

Suddenly I'm sitting on the window ledge, hands pressed against cold glass. Mojo is gone, and so is Anna. "The book." It must have been a dream, I think, it had to be. Unless I left it behind. My heart sinks.

I can't get Mojo out of my head, the way he looked at me, his dark promises, the things he did to my sister. I walk to my bookcase, rub my hands over bindings, over book tops. Something falls to the floor. It's the book, torn and tattered. It must have been in my collection all the time. I crack open the book, the words *Spell of Reversal* jump out at me. I close the book and gasp as I look at the withered cover.

In spidery writing scrawled across the face of the book, is the name Mojo DeCanne.

25

The book has beauty in it, but also contains dark and unthinkable things. I think of Daniel's grandmother and her Manhattan grimoires. There are spells for love, for protection and for wealth, penned in lovely flowery writing. Perhaps Anna's, I'm not sure. And then there's information about summoning demons to murder your enemies, to steal the souls of the innocent and give them to a dark master. There is a torn page where instructions are given about how to call the dead from Hell. The remainder of it is glued to one of my sister's collages. I've put them together, read the awful words and know why DeCanne wants it back. Allie must have stolen the whole book, torn out the page. I read, listen to my heart pound in my chest…

On any night, no need to wait for a full moon, for that is old witch superstition, you can call the demons. Simply find a creature with blood like your own, someone with skin like yours. If someone has died and that person was bad then you can turn around the spell my son has cast. Cut out his heart and offer it to the night, to the Master and say: Open your hell gates and free your servants, the murderers and all those who have defiled the Earth. Make them walk here again so that they may serve you under my command.

I place the book on the window ledge and look to the top of the building. I swear a dark figure watches me through blinding snow and that at any moment he'll crash through window glass and take back his treasure. I feel Daniel's arms around me as his lips brush the back of my neck. His voice is sleepy and sexy. "You OK? Thought I heard voices, something—"

"Daniel, the top floors, somebody could've gotten to Lilly and the others by opening a window and climbing down the fire escape. Did you—"

"I climbed up to the top, almost broke my neck on the ice. I tried every window, ones near ledges, near fire escapes, wherever possible. Windows are all nailed shut from the outside. Nobody, but nobody got in or out. Believe me."

I look to the top of the building, to snow-covered ledges, to the ice-glazed and rickety fire escape. I sigh. "You could have gotten killed."

"I've been in worse situations." He turns me around, looks in my eyes then pulls me close and kisses me hard. "Wake me if you need me."

I say nothing, just wait for him to leave me then I turn my attention to the window I climbed through with Anna in my dream. I see her again, waving, smiling at me, beckoning for me to join her, and I don't know how, but now I'm standing before the window. It isn't nailed shut as Daniel promised. It's open and snow is melting on the stained wooden floor inside.

I climb inside, walk gingerly through the empty room and push open the splintered door.

Voices whisper to me from dark corners. Shadows waver and sway on the walls. All doors are ajar and people roam the hallways like ghostly specters. Their clothing is soiled and torn. No one looks my way as they drift from doorway to doorway in silence. Footsteps sound behind me. I bolt up a flight of stairs. Breathless, I lean on the banister, stare in awe at a man sprawled out on the landing. Blood trickles from his mouth.

I climb another flight. A man and woman lay together at the foot of the stairs. He is slowly climbing on top of her, pushing her dress to her waist then rocks back and forth. The woman stares straight ahead, her mouth slack, eyes glazed.

I back away slowly until I move into a room. It's so cold in here. I hold several brown paper bags in my arms, but have no recollection of picking them up. It's then that I realize I'm dreaming again.

Mojo DeCanne sits at a table. A platter and oversized silverware piled beside it sits before him.

"What is this place?"

He motions to the table, and though I don't want to, I obediently move to his side and hand him the bags.

"Bad part of town," he says through a wicked grin, tearing open the brown paper. He removes containers, greedily spoons rice and chicken into his mouth. After a moment he stops, rummages through the boxes until he finds whatever he's looking for, then carefully lifts it out and gently places it on the plate. A heart, a human heart, still beating somehow. He smothers it with rice. "This place was once a bordello. When the girls got too old I'd bring them to the church in Harlem and offer them up for one trinket or another. Can't get much for used goods like that, but they're still human souls, still good for certain commodities."

He continues to stir his food, and I can see the heart beating, rice and blood spilling onto the table. Mojo laughs. It is a hideous sound. "Lots of shit went down here in the 70's. Dope, crap like that. There was a weird cult here in the 80's." He puts his finger to his chin. "People die here all the time. It's a bad place." He smacks his lips. "My family still owns this rat hole, relatives somewhere else in the city—or maybe in Florida—I've forgotten. They have strict instructions never to open up the top floors."

"There were people in the hallway having sex. The woman, she looked—"

"Yeah, she sure did." Blood drips from his chin, stains his teeth. "Eat something."

I want to back away, but can't.

"We both know what you came here for. A little spin in the hay with DeCanne and then you give me back what's mine."

"Is this how you got to my sister? Were you in her dreams too?"

A black bird perches outside the window, pecks on the snowy pane as if answering for him then flies away. Blood smears the glass.

DeCanne reaches over, touches my hand. His flesh is hot, alive. "Lay down." He smells of old sweat, of rotting city alleys and of things indescribable and evil.

"I'd rather die."

"Oh, you will, Gina. You will."

"This is only a—I'm dreaming, I'm only dreaming. You can't hurt me."

He smacks his lips again. "A lonely sad little chick walked through the alley a few nights back. She got knifed by a junkie. I saw the whole thing. She's on the fifth floor now. Only she's not lonely anymore." His fingers crawl from my hand to my arm, wrap around my elbow. When he releases me a red smear stains my forearm. "The dead and the damned got to go somewhere. This is one place they come once they realize there's no hope. It never stops, they just keep coming, and time swallows them whole."

Finally, able to move, I bolt from the room. People are lined up in the hallway. They don't look human in gathering shadows. Their faces are too white, their bodies distorted. Feral cats weave in and out between their spindly legs.

The dead guests bend down, pet the cats and smile as guttural growls fill the hallway.

"Gina," they call, reaching for me as I pass.

More wait for me on the landing, their demon faces leering, elongated fingers burning my flesh.

A woman steps out of the crowd and kisses me. "I can make love to you," she whispers, "is that what you want?" Half her face is missing and the fingers on her left hand have been severed. Her right arm dangles from her shoulder by thin tendrils of flesh. "My name's Bella. I was a lot like you, I can—"

I stagger away, keep running.

A skeletal black man with dreadlocks and a Bible in his hand emerges from the center of the crowd. His mouth splits into a wide toothless smile. "Nobody can save you now."

I squeeze shut my eyes, bring my hands to my head and cover my ears. "Get away!"

I'm holding the book. It's open to a page with beautiful and flowery writing and Anna's voice is in my head. "If someone has died and that person was bad then you can turn around the spell my son has cast. Cut out the heart and..."

"Good book?" Daniel is awake again, standing in front of me and smiling. "Looks old."

I look around. I'm awake too, the dream and its demons gone. "It's *interesting*," I tell him.

He takes the book from me, puts it on the window ledge then pulls me to my feet and kisses me. "Wish things were different."

"One day," I say softly, "maybe they will be."

I nestle into the warmth of his arms and wish the storm and the dreams it's sent to haunt me would end.

I suddenly find myself thinking about Dave Sousa and how he

was in life, how he taunted me, how he got a friend of mine fired last spring. People said he didn't call 911 when his father complained about chest pains during a hunting trip they took together a few years back. He let the old man die then inherited all his money. Nobody could prove a thing, but the cops suspected. I think about Anna's words, *"If someone has died and that person was bad then you can turn around the spell my son has cast."*

A vision of a woman straddling Dave's body and cutting his heart out with a large ornate dagger blinks in my mind's eye. When the woman stops and looks back over her shoulder at me, I realize I'm watching myself.

Daniel sighs and releases his hold on me, and I can't be certain if it's because he's somehow seen the horrible dark things that fill my mind, or if those same demons are now tormenting him too.

26

"I had a dream about my grandmother," Daniel says softly. "I have the same dream a lot. She's in her bedroom in the old house where she lived, surrounded by these odd dolls she used to make, some with pins and charms stuck in them. She has books spread out on her bed and she's crying, telling me she's always with me, always there in spirit. There's another woman behind her, and, it's hard to explain, but it's like I know this woman, and yet, I don't."

"Anna, her name is Anna," I tell him. "Her picture's in that book. She's Mojo's mother."

Daniel's eyes widen. "She told me that in the dream." He waves his hand, as I've seen him do many times now when he chooses to dismiss something. "Coincidence," he says, and pulls his cell phone from his pocket. "We've got to be rational." He punches a number into the phone and suddenly smiles. "Holy shit, it went through, it's ringing."

"Please let someone pickup." I cross my fingers for emphasis, like I did when I was a child.

Daniel puts a hand over his left ear to block out noise, and presses the phone tighter against his other ear. He moves away from me and into the hall, probably hoping for a better signal there. I hear him tell someone what's happened here. I hear the words "forensics" and "homicides." "They're coming," he tells me as he crosses back into the room. "Hold tight, girl."

A rush of relief surges through me, and I'm suddenly elated that we won't be alone in this death house much longer. I go to the window, no longer afraid that an evil magic man may be lurking in the street or leering at me from a window above. "Snow's finally stopping."

"City's coming back to life," he says with a weary smile. "They told me plows have cleared the main avenues and that a few stores are opening so people can get food."

I try to imagine just how bad it must be out there, how enormous and deadly the storm must have been to shut down a city like New York. I wonder how many other dramas played out across the city during this brutal dark night, and how countless others must also be hopefully awaiting rescue.

For several minutes Daniel and I remain quiet, reflecting on what's happened and what might still be to come. Emotionally, mentally and physically exhausted, we decompress just a few feet from each other, needing to do this alone in our own individual spaces for some reason. It's been a hellish night, and somehow we've survived it, and there is an odd satisfaction in that, in still being alive despite the odds, but it is mixed with heavy sorrow for the others, and for the evil that still lurks out there in the snow, in the shadows beyond the light of a new day.

I hear sirens and voices downstairs sometime later. An internal switch apparently thrown, Daniel snaps out of his reflection and heads for the door. "Got work to do," he tells me flatly. "Stay here."

I nod and think of Dave's body sprawled on the floor. They'll take him away and I won't be able to do what I need to do. I sigh and shake my head. "You're fucking crazy," I mutter. "It was all just a dream, a nightmare. A flesh and blood killer is on the loose, not some dead man from your imagination."

Policemen and criminal scientists talk downstairs, and I hear Daniel recounting the details of what we went through. Then I hear a new voice, rich and deep. "Heard it on my police scanner."

"Sir, this is a crime scene," someone tells this intruder, "we're going to need you to step outside and we can—"

"I'm Martin DeCanne, the owner of this building. I have every right to be here."

That voice is familiar.

I walk to the landing, look down then move slowly down the stairs. Somebody is examining Dave's chest wound, swabbing blood and God knows what else. He's stoic, cold and detached as he puts his death samples in a box and then gets up and walks away.

"As the owner of this property, I have rights." DeCanne, an

African-American man in his mid-thirties, talks to Daniel but looks rather suddenly up at me. His eyes are like Mojo's, and I remember the dream and how relatives still own the building.

My fear returns.

Martin is still speaking, saying something I can't quite make out. There is a smile on his face when he reaches into his pocket, removes a gun and points it at Daniel. The blast is loud, and the building shakes as a spray of blood spatters the wall. Daniel vaults backward and falls.

People are moving quickly, taking loudly, some surrounding Daniel, but I can no longer see Martin DeCanne. Everyone has gone insane, yelling, telling me to go back upstairs. Stunned and still not able to fully comprehend what's happened, I do as they tell me, moving slowly and sluggishly back up the stairs. "Daniel?"

With my ears ringing from the gun blast, I go to the kitchen, open a drawer and remove a carving knife. What I have to do is insane—and I know it—but that can no longer stop me from what I now know *has* to be done. I get one of my oversized purses from the closet then walk slowly through the hall, through the living room and toward the landing. No one is near Dave. Someone says Martin got away. Cops are running out of the building, getting into police cars, others move down the street on foot searching for him. The CSI people have collected their samples and have gone up the stairs, searching for clues. No one seems to notice me.

I kneel down near Dave. His eyes are open and drool runs a path down his cheek. He grabs my arm. "You're dead, you fucker. You're fucking dead."

I look down at him again and his eyes are shut. His hands are by his sides. I take a deep breath then plunge the knife into his already damaged chest. As bile bubbles up into the back of my throat I choke it down and begin to cut, severing the heart from the surrounding arteries. Gagging, I place the knife by his side and slowly lift the organ. Cupping it gently in my trembling hands, I ease it into my purse.

No one's here now except Daniel and some paramedics who are working hard to save him. As I move closer I see them leaned over him, blocking my view.

"It's ok," I tell him softly, even though he may already be dying.

My shock and sorrow has already turned to rage and determination, reminding me of what must be done, of what I must do.

I will end all of this once and for all, or I'll die in the attempt and take my chances on the other side with Mojo DeCanne and his devils.

Unnoticed, I clutch my bloodstained purse to my chest, and step out into the snow.

27

I'm not wearing a coat or gloves, and the temperature on the marquee at the corner store reads fifteen degrees Fahrenheit. I should be freezing, but there's too much adrenaline pumping through me to feel anything but rage and hatred for the man who shot Daniel, for Mojo himself. I need to get to the church. Anna was there when I cut out the heart. She showed me things I couldn't understand until now. I know what I need to do. I saw her pouring the blood from Dave's heart over the altar, throwing dead flower petals into the crimson puddles left behind and then burying the evil thing in snow piled against the church's cold stone exterior. She told me, "Do as I've shown you and the world will be safe from Mojo, from Martin." A few people walk down the normally bustling Avenue, but don't seem to notice me standing here on the apartment stairs. I wait until they reach the corner before I step onto the walk, not even sure where to begin.

I can't drive my car. The streets are treacherous. The buses or subways are probably shut down. How the hell am I going to get to Harlem? Something in my gut tells me I'm meant to go back to the church and that someway, somehow, I'll get there. I look to the snow at my feet, see something shining within the white. I bend down. There's a tiny charm, a caged bird, red with silver speckles, glimmering in the snow. I pick it up, unable to stop staring at it. I once lost a similar charm in the snow, when I was kid, still in grammar school, and looking at this one now brings me back to when Allie and I used to walk to the corner drugstore after supper every night.

The place was run by an elderly couple who kept the store well supplied with sweets and penny candy. It was furnished with an old-fashioned soda fountain where ice cream sodas and fries were served on shiny counters, and there was a bubble gum machine set on that counter filled with fat balls of gum for only a nickel each. A little plastic charm always accompanied the gum. Allie and I lived for those things, had boxes filled with them. On a cold December evening, a little charm, red and speckled with silver, fell into my open hand after I'd plunked in my money and turned the machine handle. I stuck it in my pocket, happy with the beautiful treasure I'd gotten. We drank sodas and giggled when a couple high school boys, tan and donned in tight jeans, strolled into the store. "I'll take that one," Allie whispered in my ear when the taller of the two smiled in our direction. "In your dreams," I whispered back, motioning to a long-legged cheerleader that strolled into the store and hooked her arm through the boy's.

Undaunted, we finished our sodas then spent an hour or more checking out comic books lined up in wooden holders at the rear of the store. When the black and white clock above the soda fountain read seven we quickly paid for the books we wanted and made our way home, giggling, pushing each other playfully and having the kind of innocent and carefree fun neither of us would ever truly know again. Our father was waiting at the door for us, and as always, he scolded us for taking so long, his eyes twinkling, probably remembering he'd done the same when he was a kid. When I got up to my bedroom I reached inside my pocket. The charm was gone. It snowed that night and snowy weather continued on and off for the next several weeks. The walks remained snow-covered and icy until a thaw, until another evening when Allie and I ventured to our favorite store. I always looked at my feet when I walked, and that night I watched the melting snow trickle off the walk and into the gutters. I found my little charm I'd lost atop a mound of snow. It was as perfect and shiny as when it had tumbled into my hand weeks before.

I wonder what happened to that little charm. Could this be the same one? Could Allie have put it here so I'd find it? Maybe she'd saved it all these years and waited for this moment so I would remember her, remember us.

As the memories fade, I am unsure of how long I've been standing on the empty street. I push the charm into my pocket and look at my blood-soaked purse. Somebody's going to call the police if they see this. There's a newsstand a block away and I walk toward it quickly. I turn to see if anyone is following me and notice a trail of crimson behind me. My stomach turns. I swear I can feel the heart pulsing.

There's no one at the newsstand, just papers piled high. A plastic raincoat hangs on a hook behind the counter. I try reaching for it, but can't quite get it.

A long arm suddenly reaches past me and unhooks the coat. "I've been looking for you, girl."

I spin on my heels. "Rico! How did you—"

He gently slides my purse off my shoulder then wraps it inside the yellow slicker. He smiles, but his eyes are sad. "They released me, told me they had new evidence. Told me everything they had on me proved to be a setup. No apologies, though. They gave me bus money and told me to get lost. Fuckers, I should sue them."

"I've got to get to the church. Sue them later."

He chuckles softly. "Anna told me everything. I know what happened to the cop too."

"You heard about Daniel?"

"Harris? Yeah, he got shot. I also know they found a room full of shit way upstairs in your apartment house, notebooks filled with stuff about how to plant evidence on suckers like me. They sacrificed people for years, made it look like murder and then set people up. Fucking city. How long has this gone on? Think of all the sick ways some people have died over the years. Could all be related to DeCanne, to his sick rituals." He holds the raincoat close to him. "Damn if I can't feel this thing beating."

"You know what it is?" I ask, barely able to believe it myself.

"I slept a lot in jail. Anna DeCanne visited me in dreams. I know what you did, and I know what needs to be done."

"The church," I say softly.

He nods, motions to a yellow cab parked across the street I hadn't realized was occupied until just then. The driver looks kind but exhausted, and seems to know Rico. He rolls down his window. "I'm going to 150th, no farther."

"Perfect." Rico takes my hand and leads me to the cab. "Nice guy. He was stuck outside Rikers when I got out. I helped him get out of the deep snow. He's determined to get home. We almost got killed a few times in this shit, but we're here. We made it. He needs to get back to his family in Harlem, make sure they're OK." Rico opens a door, I slide in and he gets inside behind me.

"If I didn't love my wife and kid so much I'd still be sitting outside that prison," the driver tells me. "Rico here is good people. He helped me. I'll help him. Only fair."

He pulls onto the street and begins creeping his way through the treacherous remnants of the storm. We see an occasional plow, police cruiser, state or city vehicle and some other cars, but they are few and far between. Most vehicles lie trapped in the snow or buried in the enormous drifts on the sides of the road, and there are barely any people on foot. The famously exciting and vibrant metropolis that is New York City has been reduced to an alien frozen landscape sparsely inhabited by beings emerging from a lengthy hibernation. It doesn't seem possible such a great and strong city like this could be so crippled. But then, nothing seems real anymore.

The driver looks at me in the rear-view mirror. "What happened to your coat? You must be freezing."

"I don't—"

Rico interrupts and tells the driver where we want to go. The driver shakes his head. "I could take you to a shelter instead. You even got money? It doesn't matter. This storm fucked up a lot of lives."

"Church is good," Rico says pleasantly. "Just get us there, and thank you."

The driver nods and doesn't say another word as we move through Manhattan, through the labyrinth of white and toward a place where even more madness waits to greet us.

Rico hands me the bundle containing Dave's heart. I move my hand over yellow vinyl and I wonder if Daniel is dead or alive.

28

Trucks spread sand on the avenue, and police cars are parked at corners. Pedestrians are few, but those I see are wrapped from head to toe in scarves and bulky coats, faces covered as they plod through snow, carrying brown bags perhaps filled with needed staples, milk, bread and pet food. I wonder if what lies beneath layers of cloth, wool and knitted things hides evil in one form or another. Perhaps the storm has stripped away, or frozen, most of what's good in this city and now only those who have come here from Hell walk these streets. Maybe Rico and I were spared because we're truly evil as well. I've wished people dead who have hurt me. I've lusted for men who were bound to others. My soul has a dark tinge to it, something not evident on the surface, but it lurks there. It torments me, and sometimes I whisper prayers learned in catechism and suffer because I will never be the saint I'd wanted to be as a child. Rico has cheated and scammed his share of tourists and naïve women looking for affordable designer handbags to show off. He's dealt drugs and gambled with his soul. Maybe we deserve to join Mojo on a path of destruction and cruelty, his children, born into this world to spread his diseased message.

The storm played out in Mojo's favor. I wonder if he conjured magic to change weather patterns, to cripple the city, to bring Rico and me to this moment in time. Could any of that be possible? Could he really be so powerful? My logical mind tells me how silly that all is, and yet somewhere deep inside me, I feel differently. Maybe anything is possible.

Rico turns to me as though he's read my thoughts. "None of us are perfect, you know. Being human means we think things and want things and sometimes do things that ain't all pure, but we get lots of chances to shape up. We try but beat ourselves up when we fail. That's what being flesh and blood is all about. People like the DeCannes are different. They don't want to change. They got no guilt, no remorse. But we do, and we gotta fight this, Gina."

"Hope you're right," I tell him.

He nods then gazes at a couple walking past a bodega. They're old and bent over and I wonder if this is the last winter they'll be on this earth. I wonder if they've erased the darkness from their souls. Does anyone ever die without it?

"Turn left then take a sharp right," Rico tells the cabbie. "Pull up alongside the church."

The driver's tired eyes find mine in the rear-view mirror. "Bad place. Real bad. Maybe I take you to my house. My wife can make soup. You can sleep in the spare room, my older son's room. He's in Iraq. He's—"

"No, man," Rico touches the thick plastic separating us from the man. "But thanks anyway. We'll be OK, I promise."

The cab pulls up to the curb. The driver gazes at the church, quiet pain in his eyes. "Devil DeCanne killed my grandmother in that place. Old woman believed he could cure her cancer. He cut it out of her belly. Butcher. People say he's buried in the cemetery in back of the church. Every time I pass by I want to stop and spit on his grave."

The driver looks back at us. "DeCanne's ghost is there. I've seen it."

"Yeah, he goes downtown a lot too," I mumble through a smirk.

Rico pushes me towards the door, unlatches it and guides me onto the snowy walk.

The driver makes the sign of the cross then pulls away, leaving us alone in this desolate part of the city. The church is ominous, looming over us like an ancient beast, ready to crumble and crush us on this Harlem street. Snow and ice cover its ancient stone. Cracked gargoyles carved into the doorframe glare at us like sentries. I notice something I've never seen before. A lone statue sits at the top of the frame, hands spread and seeming to call the other figures into his fold. The Devil, with two women chained to his wrists, a figure I've seen in Tarot decks, but in the decks the chains don't bind and the Tarot's subtle symbolism implies that we create our own bondage, that we can free ourselves if we try. I have a feeling we won't get off so easy. DeCanne's chains bind forever.

We walk across the snowy walk, making our way to the stairs. Wind erupts and snow tumbles from canopies sheltering windows above. I imagine the Devil bending and brushing my face with crooked fingers, but it's only dark shadows made by birds flying overhead, by the sun moving in and out of gray clouds. I step back and look up at the King of Demons. He's silent, still a creature carved from stone, but I'm sure evil spirits reside in him. I'm sure old Mojo rubbed potions all over him and said incantations before he was placed above the door. I know everything and anything Mojo did was for a reason, all of them evil and vile.

Rico turns to me, "Ready?"

I nod.

I remove the yellow slicker from my purse, watch it fall to the sidewalk and then I drape the blood-soaked satchel over my shoulder.

"Lead the way." My voice cracks.

Rico's fingers touch the door, and as it creaks open, I think about Daniel. The voices of the dead stop whispering whatever it was they were whispering before our intrusion. I hope Daniel's not among them. Have they rushed him off to a hospital where he's now being cared for, or has a coroner already pronounced him dead and carted him away in a body bag?

The door opens easily, and those mammoth saints tower above us, eyes seeming to mock, lips seeming to move slowly as we walk past. Joan of Arc pulls her shoulders back and raises her sword, but it's just candlelight creating an illusion. It's got to be. I jump slightly when something-someone-touches my arm, but I tell myself it's only my imagination. There's something under a rack of burning candles, wrapped in a dirty rag, with brown liquid stains. It rolls slightly and part of the cloth moves. An eye peeks through the opening and I flinch.

"He's in our heads," Rico whispers. "I-I'm seeing stuff."

"Me too."

"Ignore it, girl, none of it's real. If we believe it he'll have us."

"OK, OK," I say as I look beneath the candle rack. It's just a dirty rag. It's all right.

Rico puts his arm through mine and guides me through the entranceway. His face is stoic. His free hand curls into a fist, and I feel his heart pounding as we move closer together. Smells of candle wax, sweet incense, flowers and dampness permeate the area.

We move inside the church itself. It's empty, but something invisible, something wicked and damned is present. I can feel it. Snow falls from the broken skylight, shimmering as it catches candlelight and melting as it touches the water-soaked floor. Moisture drips from walls and for a moment it looks as though blood is trickling down wooden carvings and marble replicas hanging there. The tin can of coffee, Allie's brew, is now overturned and at the feet of a statue of Michael the Archangel. His spear points downward as if about to attack, and the serpent at his feet is curled around his legs, its sharp fangs biting into his right ankle. Angels at the altar do not look angelic. Their eyes are tinged with red and their fingers are distorted. Is this how they were sculpted and created, or has Mojo DeCanne altered them for his own purposes?

"Is this Hell?" I ask Rico as I look toward the splintered wooden crucifix. It's different too. Someone has inverted it and the sad and tortured Christ has been replaced by a bloody skeleton. The bones are broken in many places. There is still flesh on the face and one eye dangles from its socket.

Dark things flank banisters on the second level, bat wings flutter and shining green eyes glare down at us from the shadows.

He sighs heavily. "As close as you'll ever be to the place, I imagine."

"Gina and Rico in Wonderland." I try to laugh but nothing comes out, my fear strangles it to silence in the base of my throat.

"Even Alice didn't have to deal with this kind of crazy. I'd rather have tea with the white rabbit any day. She would've been playing a different tune if she had the DeCanne clan fucking with her, I'll tell you that."

Somehow our silly banter distracts us enough to keep us moving deeper into the church.

"You shoulda brought a camera," Rico says, "recorded as much of this as you could."

A harsh wind seems to come from nowhere and the temperature seems to drop at least ten degrees. One of the angels smiles slowly, and blood trickles from her lips. Insane laughter erupts from the rafters above. Martin DeCanne glares at us from there and he laughs again. The laughter rises to a high pitch then wanes. He's silent for several seconds as though gathering his thoughts before he speaks. "My great grandfather left a legacy for me. He left me magic, his books; his life's work. I learned a lot of tricks and I've brought him back through me. He's inside me, working his magic. He's in this city, resurrecting followers from forgotten graves" He smiles at me. "He sees potential in people like you. The living can cause such havoc if they're trained well. I choose you." He points at me then slowly moves his aim to Rico.

"You're a mortal man, just like me," Rico shouts. "You're just insane."

"Could be, little Rico, could be. But insanity gives you power, makes you fearless, sets you free." DeCanne walks as he speaks, moves towards the stairs then slowly begins to descend them. "Rico, you have your father's blood in you. How close have you come to killing? He'd already murdered a man at your age. I think you're on the verge. All you need is a little help, a little push. What about the lover that left you? How many times have you plotted to follow him, find him and strangle him with your bare hands?"

"It's just human emotion. I'd never..." I feel Rico shaking when he speaks.

"He's just a man," I whisper, "nothing more." DeCanne stops then sweeps his hands back and forth in one grand gesture.

Black birds spiral from somewhere behind him and fly toward us. They scream and beat their wings like devil drums, seemingly coming from within him. He looks directly at me. "Just like the dreams, Gina, just like the things inside your head."

"It's an illusion," Rico says as beady black bird eyes stare into mine, their sharp beaks tearing at my clothes. "Gina, tell yourself it's not real."

One of the birds bites into my cheek and I feel warm blood gush down my face; see it trickle onto my hand. "You're not real!" I scream, wishing the hell birds away.

And then there's silence.

I touch my face but find no blood there, no damage. I look toward DeCanne and say. "Go back to Hell with your great grandfather. Go back where you fucking belong."

"Not so easy," he says, waving his hands once more. Demon things with hooked claws and tongues studded with sharp blades appear. "Tell me these aren't real. My great grandpa gave them to me. Now I'm giving you to them."

"You're fucking ridiculous," I tell him, tension firing through my body. "You look like something out of a B-movie."

"Gina, Gina, Gina. Your sister dared to be and do things you only dream about. You were jealous of her, no? Growing up you wished she'd fall from the apple tree she dared to climb. Later you wished the Harley her boyfriend drove would veer out of control and crash. I hear *all* your prayers, bitch."

A woman manifests before DeCanne. On her knees, a knife in hand, she cuts her face. But it isn't until she looks up at me, her eyes wide and scared, that I realize it's my sister. "I want to cut it all away," she says, her voice slightly garbled. "Maybe you'll love me more if I cut all the bad away, Gina."

A lump forms in my throat and my eyes fill with tears. "Allie, no, I never meant..."

"And your mother. You were ashamed of her. You couldn't bring your friends to your house for fear she'd have one of her episodes. She couldn't sit you on her knee and read to you like a normal mother. She was too busy thinking of herself, about how bad her life was, how her demons were tearing her apart. You wished her dead and your wish came true."

Allie's image wavers then disappears, replaced with my mother, standing there now and dressed in a bloody nightgown. Her wrists and ankles are cut, crimson rivulets drip from her flesh. "Gina, Mommy did it for you, so you could have a life, have friends." My mother's face changes and Mojo DeCanne's eyes gaze into mine. "But blood is blood and you're just as insane as she was, just as insane as your sister. And you wished them both dead. You're the most evil of all."

"It wasn't my fucking fault, you sonofabitch, I—"

"Don't listen to him," Rico shouts at me. "Don't listen!"

The visions vanish, leaving only Martin DeCanne visible through the darkness, smoke and shadows. He laughs and waves his finger back and forth as ashes drift in the place where his demons once stood. He smiles a slow, wide, hideous smile and removes a dagger from his coat. The hilt is shaped like a dragon's head, the eyes red rubies. "The dragon. He's magical, fiercely passionate, a symbol of strength. Some would say I've perverted this strength, made it unclean." He steps a few steps closer. "But I have my reasons."

Rico takes my arm, gently guides me backward as he speaks. "Look man, the cops will figure it out. They know it's you. They saw you shoot the cop back at the apartment."

Still grinning demonically, DeCanne points the dagger at us. "You think *cops* concern *me*?"

"There's evidence, a trail way too big you've left," Rico tells him. "You won't get away with it, man, not this time." DeCanne strokes the dagger with sexual glee. "No one cares about either of you. You're both rotten to the core, just like me. Ready to die, children?"

I scream Rico's name but DeCanne is already on the move, leaping forward like a feral cat and flying at us as no human being ever could.

As he lands he knocks Rico down and I hear him cry out. I stagger away, trying to keep my balance as blood trickles to the floor around me. Rico's blood. I fight off the instinctual desire to run because there's no point. I could never outrun DeCanne and he'd only pull me down from behind and stab me in the back. But I know if I stand here and do nothing he'll kill me for sure.

I spin around, trying to find DeCanne again. And then he's right there, eyes fastened on mine, mocking me. "It'll be slower for you," he whispers. "Much slower."

He moves towards me with inhuman speed, clamps his clammy hand onto my wrist and begins dragging me toward the altar. He's so strong my resistance does little to stop him and I stumble along after him like a child in the throes of a tantrum.

The church around me is a blur as the eyes of saints and sinners watch in passive silence and the dark things along the ceiling lift their wings and float above us, buzzards waiting for death's inevitable arrival and their turn to feast on all that remains.

I fall, crash into the altar where I'm thrown. DeCanne looms over me, the dagger to my throat. "Nice and slow," he whispers. "I'm going to cut that dark part of your soul out and feed it to you. As it grows and becomes stronger, we'll nurture it, mixing it with your blood. And when it's reached its full power and you're nothing but a hollowed out husk of what you once were, I'll send you to Hell with my great grandfather like the piece of shit on the bottom of my shoe you are."

A fleeting memory plays out before me. Daniel kisses me, gently makes love to me. Daniel, sweet Daniel, I could have loved you so much. Where are you now? A soft voice sounds in my head. "I'm so sorry." Anna DeCanne kneels beside me, seemingly appearing from nowhere. She looks to Martin. "Stop this now. The magic I taught your great grandfather was never meant for this lunacy."

DeCanne's eyes water as he reaches for her.

"Stop," she says, and pulls away. "Stop this, Martin. Stop this."

He wipes his eyes and shakes his head. "Too late, it's...it's too late now."

The dagger shines and the rubies on its hilt seem to come alive. Layers of spells, of souls murdered and captured inside rare gems flicker before my eyes. Mojo's dark eyes stare back at me, full of hate. And then I know I'll never leave this awful place alive. Anna clicks her tongue, touches me gently. "Don't give up. I'm the reason why you're here and I'm the only one who can deal for you now." She waves her hand and I see a young girl standing in a playground. She's crying and her dress is torn. Her beautiful black hair shines under radiant beams of sunlight filtering through the leaves of tropical trees. The girl sobs harder as she watches other children play catch and a game of chase. But then the scene changes. Green leaves turn dark and brittle, and the sun no longer shines. The same girl, a few years older now, lies on bloody sheets, screaming as a hooded woman bends over her and mumbles words in another language. The words come faster and faster as she bends deep between the crying girl's legs. Within moments a baby emerges, dark and covered with crimson clots. She quickly wraps him in a black shawl. Turning back to the shivering girl, she closes her eyes and whispers, "Bad omen, this child, born during the darkest part of the eclipse." The woman opens her eyes, reveals black glistening orbs, no longer human. "God help you, Anna."

"Alone," Anna says, speaking slowly, deliberately, "from the time I was a child, always alone and mocked by others, left to bear my son in shame—alone again. I learned the magic from the very woman who helped bring Mojo into this world, and I swore I'd do good with it, never evil. But he wanted revenge because he loved me so much. He swore he'd make humanity pay for his mother's suffering, for their cruelty."

DeCanne, crying again, tears streaming down his otherwise maniacal face, waves the dagger near my face. "I'll cut the darkness out, I—I'll cut it all out."

"No, Martin." Anna moves between us and gently takes my hand in hers. "*No.*"

Falling...I see her falling away from me through a tunnel glimmering with white light...or is it only snow falling, cascading down upon me from a broken skylight?

Am I dead already?

I hear whispers somewhere nearby—prayers or chants, I can't be sure which as they're not in a language I recognize—then the light slips away and returns me to darkness.

And whatever waits for me there.

29

I once read about how after death you shed your physical body and enter another plane or dimension. Where you go depends on how you lived your life, the things you thought about and how you treated others. I haven't been perfect. I cursed Dave and look what happened to him. I admit I was jealous of my sister at times, wishing she'd just disappear so I'd get more attention. I even admit I was ashamed of my mother. I've done other things too. I once made a doll out of rags and yarn and called it Mrs. Redding (after a Math teacher in my senior year of high school). Throughout the year I'd stick a pin in the doll each time Mrs. Redding gave me a less than average grade. She was a robust woman in September. By October she'd lost her double chin. In November, her bones poked through her arms and wrists and right before Christmas break she passed out in front of the class. She never returned to school. In the spring, I heard she was slowly and painfully dying in a cancer ward at the old state hospital. In May she died. I threw the doll in a box beneath my bed, pins and all, but for months I'd dream about her screaming in some hellish place, throwing test papers in the air—my test papers—and begging me to take out the pins. I finally did remove them and buried the doll beneath the bright yellow Queen Elizabeth roses in my father's garden, dappling the grave with holy water I took from a font at the local parish church. The dreams stopped, but Mrs. Redding was still dead.

I could be dead now, I know this. I could be on one of those dark planes I read about, where vibrations are low, where demons reside. My feet tingle and my hands are numb. I hear voices, some swearing, others telling me how much pain they're suffering.

I see myself as I pass a mirror, one with hissing serpents creeping around its frame and bones dangling from its edges. I look closely and see I'm drenched with blood, my face sliced with flesh rivulets. I am filled with rage when I hear Mojo's voice. "Give me back what's mine, bitch." I see a shadow, even darker than the deepest blacks in this place...just before I feel his breathe on the back of my neck. I gaze at myself once more. The bloody bag containing Dave's heart is still draped over my shoulder.

"Did you hear what I said?" Mojo grabs me, spins me around. We are both suddenly engulfed in an inferno. Orange flames lick at our bodies while lost souls scream in agony beneath us. Yet neither of us burn. He smiles, staring deeply into my eyes, "Your sister's down there, you know. I had her so many times I even came back through Martin just so I could fuck the shit out of her again." I remember the dream I had of Allie, blood spurting from between her legs.

Reading my mind, Mojo laughs. "Your friend Rico's down there too." He leans in closer to me so his lips nearly touch the side of my face. "And so is your heartthrob Daniel. He's not the saint you think he is."

"All you tell are lies." My hands, feet and body slowly regain feeling. The cuts on my face hurt and my back feels as though someone has broken it in two. The weight of my bloody satchel intensifies as I gaze into Mojo's hateful eyes. "I'm not listening to them, not anymore."

"I'm the only one you've got to listen to, bitch. I'll tell you stories about the world you left behind and year after year you'll cry when you think about your beloved city and all the things you could've done."

"You're dead," I tell him. "And once Martin dies, once they give him the needle for what he's done, you'll never be able to walk the Earth again."

"Not true. There's always someone willing to play the game for me. The dead are a dime a dozen. I've resurrected countless numbers of them. They're already walking around up there, among the living, undetected. They'll help me whenever I say."

As the flames part, beyond more fire, I see fields of gravestones where mourners crawl on their hands and knees. They look at us, eyes bloody and dead, palms up, their flesh torn to reveal bone and blue veins. Their sadness fills me. I wish I could scoop them up, bring them to a place where there is light, where Buddha, Mary and Jesus smile with hands clasped in prayer and where the beauty of pure and sinless souls is enough to make everything OK. But nothing is OK and we drift further into Hell, over bodies hanging from splintered tree branches, hands clasped in fruitless prayer and mouths open with everlasting screams. The temperature changes and heat dissipates as we float over a place where mothers search in vain for children they will never find, in shallow graves, in rat-infested alleys and in the never-ending avenues of a snowbound city. It's freezing and it's snowing like it was the last few days I spent on Earth.

"Different levels of Hell," DeCanne tells me. "We're approaching your eternal place of agony, but I can let you go if you tell me what I want to know. Tell me where she hid my spell. Tell me now, and I'll set you free." His black eyes watch me, waiting for an answer.

I smile. It fades from my face slowly, deliberately. "Fuck you."

Mojo growls in anger, grabs my arm and pulls me down. The snow covers me quickly, stinging my wounded face, hurting my body even more. He rises upward, floats away and melts into darkness. I hear the screams of the dammed as snow clings to my hair. And then I hear his voice. "There's no way out of here."

I look to my bloody bundle. I unhook it from my shoulder. I have to work quickly.

I crouch down and attempt to open the bag, but my hands, cold and stiff, hurt terribly. I rub my palms together then lift the bottom of my sweater, place my hands on my breasts then tuck my sweater down from the inside. A bit of warmth spreads through my fingers and into my wrists. "It's OK. It's going to be OK," I tell myself, but then I hear Mojo's horrible laughter and my heart sinks. I look upward and see him descending toward me.

I slide my hands from beneath the sweater, open the bag and remove the heart. It's awful, blood congealed over dangling shreds of flesh. I swear it pulses with each beat as Dave's voice torments me. "Go fuck yourself," I tell him. I drop it on a mound of snow and begin to dig into the freezing white powder.

"Stop." Mojo is near, too near. "I command you to stop."

I throw the heart into the hole I've dug then scoop up more snow and bury it, covering it in the hopes of killing this horror and finding my way back out of Hell.

Mojo stands over me, tears stream down his face. "Unbury it now!" He gasps as clouds part and sun streams from a startling blue sky.

"Too late." I hear Anna's voice blending with sirens, blending with footsteps, with voices I know. "You're damned and so am I."

Daniel bends over me, his arm in a sling. Rico limps towards me, blood on his jacket.

"Just your arm? It's only your arm?" I say to Daniel. "And, you. You're alive," I say to Rico. I blink and realize neither Daniel or Rico are really there. I hear sirens and think perhaps they're taking Rico away, wonder if Daniel is still lying on the cold floor back in my apartment building.

A detective hovering over me cups my elbow. "Rico's hurt bad, not sure if he'll make it." He says nothing of Daniel and I fear he might be dead.

"Martin...Mojo," I gasp, not sure if I actually got the words out.

"Took him away," the detective says, helping me up. His eyes are stoic, filled with compassion. "It's OK. You been drinking the same kinda coffee as in that container we found here?"

"Yeah—my sister Allie—she brought it—"

"Laced with Peyote," he interrupts, "or something real similar. According to the lab guys it's most likely some strange mixture or strain of it that they haven't been able to completely identify yet. Definitely consists mostly of Peyote, though, the stuff they use in magical ceremonies. Causes hallucinations and in some cases, can simulate psychosis and even bring on psychotic episodes."

"You don't say?" I look at him blandly. "I did the spell of reversal."

"What?" the detective picks up my bag. There's no blood on it. No heart stuffed inside.

"Anna told me what to do. It's in Hell. Dave's heart is buried in the snow in Hell."

"Sure, absolutely, that makes perfect sense." The detective shakes his head. "Need to get you to the ER, pump that shit out of your system, and make sure that bastard DeCanne didn't do any physical harm."

I look to the ceiling and see Anna floating above me. Is she holding Dave's heart in her hands?

As cops and forensic scientists spread out through the church, my knees buckle and everything begins to fade. Maybe I'm not really OK after all. I wonder if Mojo DeCanne is permanently in Hell where he belongs and if Martin will spend the rest of his sorry life behind bars, maybe get the needle? Or am I the one trapped in my own Hell?

Sirens sound and I'm inside an ambulance. Rico is sitting beside me, muttering about peyote, coffee and how he saw demons inside the church. But when I reach for him, I see it's not Rico at all, just a paramedic silently taking my pulse.

I make a silent promise to be a better person, to stop making dolls with pins and to think good and positive thoughts, to get myself together and to help others. I close my eyes and begin to drift away, listening to the siren, to the sounds of a city coming alive again. I want to see Daniel and Rico. I imagine Daniel's soothing voice, then hear Rico telling jokes about handbags he's sold down on Canal Street.

It sounds so good, but something deep in my gut tells me to beware.

30

A doctor stands over me. He's wearing a spotless white coat. His hands look soft and there's compassion in his gray-blue eyes. "Your heart's racing," he tells me, "most likely due to trauma. I'm a bit concerned about your head wound."

"Head wound?" I ask. I touch my head and feel thick bandages. I don't remember being hit in the head. Did DeCanne hit me with something?

The doctor nods. "Nasty gash, slight concussion, looks like you hit the cement pretty hard. I also want to make sure the herbs you've been guzzling didn't do any permanent damage."

"The stuff in the coffee?"

He smiles sympathetically. "Yes, strange brew. Forensics is still dissecting it."

I remember dropping acid with Allie years before, and how I saw God standing by a purple waterfall. On another trip, something dark and alien tore through the ceiling and was about to swoop down on me. I screamed and Allie grabbed me, told me it was OK, that she was there and nothing could harm me. I believed her. Then.

"Do you have family, friends? We could get in touch with them.

I stop and think. My family's all gone. My ex was dead when I met him. "Rico," I say, "my friend Rico."

"The young man you were with in the church?"

I nod. "He's my only friend."

"He's in intensive care. It's touch and go right now. His doctor is doing her best."

"You *bastard*, DeCanne. It's not fucking fair."

The doctor's eyes widen, and his face reddens. He flips his chart. "You'll stay the night for observation. Do you feel up to answering some questions? A detective's been waiting. If you'd rather not, I can send him away."

I think of Daniel. "No, it's all right, I want to talk about it." Maybe Daniel's the one waiting, maybe he's OK and back on the job.

The doctor exits, his white coat billowing behind him like a cloud of white smoke. I think of angels for some reason. I wonder if they watch over me.

Someone enters the room. His hair is shoulder-length, thick waves, like Daniel's hair. He's wearing jeans and a leather jacket. "I'm Detective Barry," he says. "I didn't get a chance to introduce myself earlier. I hear you're going to be fine."

I realize he's the officer from the church.

"I'm trying. Where's Daniel—Detective Harris?"

The detective sits in a chair by the bed. "I haven't heard any news. Last I knew they were still operating on him."

"Is he here, in this hospital?"

"No, farther uptown. Listen, I'm supposed to be the one asking the questions." He smiles slightly, tips his head then speaks slowly. "What were you and your friend Rico doing up in Harlem in that God-forsaken place? Did Martin DeCanne lure you there?"

"In a way. We knew his family had a history there, a bad one, and we thought we could make things right, end a lot of bullshit by going there." I think of Dave's heart, how I brought it with me, how the blood drenched my purse.

"I know the DeCanne's are evil, that they conjure up the dead and only Anna is good, only she looked out for me."

"Anna, huh?" He shakes his head. "They found a can of that coffee you'd been drinking in the church and another in your apartment. Cops took some from Rico's place too. Where'd you guys get it?"

"My sister. She's dead."

"Any clue where she got it?"

"She knew a lot of people. Some bad, some dead."

The detective sighs heavily. "Look, I'll come back when you're more lucid."

"I can't tell you anything I haven't already told the cops about my sister. It all leads back to her—her and Mojo."

Detective Barry stands. "When you're more lucid, that's when we'll continue this conversation."

He walks away slowly, seems to fade a bit as he walks through the door. I wonder if any of this is even real. Maybe I'm really lying on an operating table fighting for my life. Maybe I'm still in Hell with Dave's blood on my hands.

I think of Allie just then, and she comes to me like a dream. We're sitting on the bed we shared when we were little. She's holding a little white pill. "You'll see God again," she laughs. "Stick out your tongue." I obey and she places the pill there.

She leans back against the bedpost. "I saw a funky Madonna last time I tripped."

I remember a series of paintings she made entitled Funky Madonna, all of a woman wearing a veil, surrounded by magic cauldrons, crucifixes, candles and statues of strange African Gods. In one painting, she held a baby. His face was sweet, eyes the deepest blue, but he had talons and fangs protruded over rosebud lips.

"I don't know where you get ideas like that."

"I see them when Mojo fucks me." She leans closer. "In Hell."

She kisses me, puts her hand on my breast. But it's not Allie, not anymore. It's a girl I saw walking in Soho one bright Sunday afternoon. She had dark hair and wore a black dress that was too tight for her. She asked me directions to a gallery on Green Street. I told her I didn't know then kept walking. I saw her every time I went to Soho after that, and I thought about her when men made love to me.

"When they made you bleed," I hear Allie say. The girl pushes her fingers into me.

Then Daniel is making love to me, gently, lovingly, the crimson between my legs gone.

Morning. It feels like I've been asleep forever. The doctor is standing over me again. "Good news. I've cleared you to be discharged today."

I look into his gray-blue eyes and see reflections of the dark-haired girl from Soho, of Anna laying out Tarot cards, of me lying by Daniel in a loft where through a window I see the East River sparkling while a full moon spills a yellow circle in its rippling water. But there, alongside it, I also see Mojo pushing me into a mound of snow, laughing insanely as he leans over to kiss me. The images melt together, play out one by one again.

"The immediate hallucinatory effects of the herb have worn off and shouldn't pose any problems we're aware of. But, we can't be entirely certain how long the drug may impact you psychologically. There is most probably something of a residual effect, as found in most hallucinatory drugs, but the extent of what that may be or how it might play out in your system specifically is something we simply don't know. All of our tests have concluded that at this point you're in good physical health and your brain has not sustained any damage due to the ingestion of the herb. However, should you experience any severe headaches, strange flashes or alteration of lights, extreme nausea, dizziness, double-vision, that sort of thing, let us know immediately, all right? If at any point you just don't feel right, or should you feel any number of unusual symptoms, such as paranoia or inexplicable anxiety, unsettling thoughts or feelings of deep depression, come back and we'll have another look at you, understand?"

I nod as the doctor scribbles something on my chart. "But I really don't expect any further problems, Gina. I think you'll be just fine."

"I can go?" I ask.

He smiles at me. "Yes, you're being discharged as we speak."

I turn away so he won't see the moisture welling in my eyes, so he won't see the truth written across my face, so he won't know that I have no idea where to go once I leave here. I want to tell him I have no idea how to even begin to resume my life, but instead I close my eyes, feel the tears trickle across my cheeks then softly say, "Thank you, Doctor."

31

"Daniel," I whisper.

When he doesn't answer I call out to Rico. Only the sounds of the city, traffic, a siren and a car horn answer.

Sitting in the dark by myself, I wonder if everyone I've loved these past few days has died. If not, if they've lived, have they abandoned me, gone on to other lives, to other friends and lovers?

"They're dead," I tell myself.

I close my eyes, try to remember Daniel's smile, Rico's laughter.

Work. I should have gone to work yesterday, or the day before, but I just sat here, lost in sorrow. I'm a guardian in this empty building where everyone has been murdered, where ghosts are trapped and confused. There are evil things on the upper floors. I know this because I've seen them, I've felt them. I know them, and they know me. I know now I have to sit here, a sentry given the task of containing the darkness that resides here. I remain on guard to prevent them from unleashing their wrath on the city I love. The doctors can talk about dope or magic herbs, crazy concoctions of hallucinogenic narcotics all they want. This has nothing to do with any of that. This building is something more...it's a portal to the demonic. I know it. The things that live here with me know it.

The phone rings. I let the answering machine take it. My boss's voice, harsh and angry, tells me not to come back. Don't worry about it, bitch, I never intended to.

I always felt a certain amount of darkness around me, desperation each time I entered this building. But it's different now. What lurks upstairs is stronger than before...meaner...but it can't get to me as long as I continue to guard the gateway...

"You have to give yourself to it," Mojo whispers. "You have to let it take you sooner or later. You're insane. You know that, don't you? You're insane, Gina, just like your mother and your sister before you, you're insane."

I push him from my mind and reach for a piece of Allie's artwork I like to keep close by. I fondly run my hand over torn paper she collaged, and for some reason it makes me think of poor Rico, all these torn pieces of paper put back together in mishmash to form something else, something different from what it had once been. Destroyed and then reassembled, but not as before, not exactly as intended.

Rico. Sweet, sweet Rico.

32

Rico sits across from me holding a steaming mug in one hand and twirling a lock of hair with the other. He's thinner than ever, slumped over a bit as though still in pain. A thick bandage is evident beneath his shirt. "Man, thanks for seeing me. Streets are tough, you know? Now more than ever."

"We got tight, shared some heavy shit."

Rico smiles, but there's something wrong. His eyes don't light up like they used to. I realize I've been holding something in my hand, Allie's miniature collage. I read the words on a torn scrap of paper. "Bring back the dead. Let them walk the Earth in my service." I sigh. "Do you know what a Grimoire is?"

"Yeah, an old magic book, sometimes wicked—sometimes not. Most times a mystery."

"I think they're hidden all over the city. I think pieces of Mojo's bad magic and pieces of stuff from people who wanted to stop it are all over fucking Manhattan. Good and evil, you know?"

Rico puts the mug down. There's blood in it, bits of flesh float at the top. "Daniel's waiting," he says. "They're all waiting. They've been waiting so long now, Gina." I reach for the cup, look into the thick vermillion then pour droplets over the art. "I made a circle of blood. Allie always did, always. Some things are just meant to be," I tell Rico as Daniel knocks on the window just like he did that day when he was checking this place out, trying to keep us safe. Only the man at the window isn't quite what he once was either. Torn to bits then hastily reconstructed. Reborn in fire as another Daniel, something like Daniel, but not quite. "We can all walk together," Rico whispers, "just like Mojo wanted. All of us, together."

Footsteps sound on the stairs, on the pavement below. The city screams with the voices of the dead. Somewhere, maybe in Heaven, things are different and I'm a different girl, but once you touch Hell, once you kiss the Devil, there's just nothing you can do to change your fate.

I leave them both there. They're already gone, already dead to me now.

I open the door to my apartment, but the stairs are empty. I descend to the ground floor, walking where dead bodies were once strewn. Upstairs, I can hear the ruckus, I can sense the darkness moving and writhing about.

Mojo and his ilk have their forces here, but so do we. Like him, I am only one of many. Fire with fire…an eye for an eye.

I think of my mother and how she endured so much, so very much. And I remember Allie, and how despite her suffering, she always seemed to know something no one else did, something that always seemed comforting to her somehow.

Beyond the front door of the building, the city pulses and moves to its own rhythm, hustles and bustles and knows nothing of what lies within these walls. It doesn't wish to know, doesn't have to know. Not yet. But that day will come. Until then, I stand vigil, stealing bits and pieces of spells and magic to keep it and its messengers at bay. Just as my mother and sister before me, I will hold off the darkness and evil until I can no longer manage it, no longer survive the madness, and then it will take me too. I will let it take me. Then just as I was chosen to follow Allie, I too will have an eventual successor.

With a smile, I gently caress my belly. It grows inside me even now, unaware of its destiny.

My child. Daniel's child.

The next guardian. The next keeper of Hell.

Something inhuman growls and then scurries off on the floor above me.

"You're insane," Mojo whispers.

With a grin some might think positively devilish, I sing a soft and loving song to my baby as I turn and slowly climb the stairs back to my apartment.

About the Author

Sandy DeLuca is an American writer and visual artist.

As an author, she is known for dark and surreal prose; often visceral and shocking. She is best known for her work in the horror genre.

She resides in New England at present, living in an old Cape Cod house, sharing that space with five felines. Her house is filled with paintings she's rendered over the years; books, ranging from popular fiction to the dark and esoteric; and an array of oddities she's purchased on journeys to New York City, Boston and Salem, Massachusetts.

She left her day job in the banking industry in 2011, and now spends her days creating fiction and painting.

Curious about other Crossroad Press books?
Stop by our site:
http://store.crossroadpress.com
We offer quality writing
in digital, audio, and print formats.

Enter the code FIRSTBOOK
to get 20% off your first order from our store!
Stop by today!

www.ingramcontent.com/pod-product-compliance
Lightning Source LLC
Chambersburg PA
CBHW061242170626
46809CB00007B/2791